Meow

Skye MacKinnon

CONTENTS

Blurb	vii
Author's Note	ix
Prologue	1
Chapter 1	16
Chapter 2	25
Chapter 3	34
Chapter 4	40
Chapter 5	47
Chapter 6	56
Chapter 7	66
Chapter 8	73
Chapter 9	83
Chapter 10	92
Chapter 11	101
Chapter 12	111
Chapter 13	120
Chapter 14	130
Chapter 15	140
Chapter 16	148
Chapter 17	157
Chapter 18	168
Chapter 19	177
Chapter 20	186
Chapter 21	193
Epilogue	203
Also By	207
About the Author	211

Meow © Copyright 2019 Skye MacKinnon

All rights reserved under the International and Pan-American Copyright Conventions. No part of this book may be reproduced or transmitted in any form or by any means, electronic or mechanical, including photocopying, recording, or by any information storage and retrieval system, without permission in writing from the publisher.

This is a work of fiction. Names, places, characters and incidents are either the product of the author's imagination or are used fictitiously, and any resemblance to any actual persons, living or dead, organizations, events or locales is entirely coincidental.

Cover by Ravenborn Covers.

Formatting by Gina Wynn.

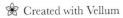 Created with Vellum

To Rachel, who kept fighting for Meow.
And to both the German and the American Lily. Keep on meowing!

BLURB

Assassin. Private Investigator. Cat shifter.

Kat is used to killing people but, for a blank cheque, she's willing to do the opposite and help solve a murder - even though it sounds boring as hell. That is, until she finds some body parts in her fridge, makes friends with the neighbourhood cats and realises there may be an assassin better than her…

Suddenly, things have become purrfectly exciting.

An urban fantasy full of cats, secrets and murders. This is a slow-burn reverse harem where Kat will find her love interests over time.

AUTHOR'S NOTE

As you will soon notice, this book is set in a world very similar to our own, but there are some deciding differences. Technology has developed differently, and while there are many devices you may be used to, such as televisions, there are no mobile phones, cars or internet. No guns, either.

This book is written in British English and uses some British expressions and idioms. Please don't see these as spelling mistakes. We say mum rather than mom, use a lot of 's' instead of 'z' (cosy, realise,…) and use 'got' as the past participle of 'get' (instead of 'gotten').

Thank you to all my Facebook followers who showed me

pictures of their cats and told me about their personalities. You'll find quite a few of these cats in this book. With these feline exceptions, all people, events and locations are fictional.

PROLOGUE

The kitten is staring at me as if I'm either a funny new toy or prey that needs killing. Maybe a little bit of both. He meows loudly, challenging me. I meow back, a hundred times louder. He looks at me in shock, then runs off, his fur ruffled in fear.

"Sorry, little one," I whisper. "I don't need any witnesses tonight."

I continue my walk along the rooftops, as silently as the kitten that I can still feel at the back of my mind. He's watching me from afar, probably wondering what the hell is going on. I'm a threat to his territory, yet he hasn't quite mustered the courage to confront me. Good. I really don't want to be distracted tonight.

I jump from one roof to the next, occasionally stopping to make sure I'm on the right track. It's much harder to orient yourself when you're on rooftops without the help of street signs and landmarks. My sense of direction is good, but I don't always trust it. That's what they taught me. Never trust anyone, not even what your mind tells you. Not what you hear, not what you see. The world is nothing but lies knitted together into a fabric that looks as if it's real.

When I reach a rooftop so old and dilapidated that even I can't help but summon a creaking sound from the broken tiles, I stop in my tracks, carefully crouching, ready to jump. I don't have much information on my mark, not nearly as much as I'd like. I don't know how strong they are and more importantly, how paranoid. Most people in this town suffer from some kind of paranoia, but some have it worse than others. Last week's first ever witch hunt in centuries is proof of that. Poor bugger.

When there's no sound from the house below, I continue on towards the dormer window. It's got an old wooden frame that looks like it's the mother of all splinters. Not going to touch that without gloves.

I take a cursory peek over the edge of the garret. No light, good. I grip the edge of the roof, pushing down on it a few times. It seems to be stable enough to hold me. Let's hope so, anyway.

Holding onto the edge with just my fingers, I let myself drop down until I'm dangling right in front of the window. According to the information I was given, this is just an attic used for storage. It should be empty. I swing back and stretch my legs out in front of me, kicking in the window as I swing forward. It's so old that it barely offers any resistance. I could have probably just pushed it in with my hands.

I drop to the floor, freezing in motion, listening to whatever's happening in the house. There's nothing but silence. He's either sleeping or not in. I hope for the former. I dread coming all the way here again. This house is at the opposite end of town from where I live. I try to avoid staying out in the open for too long. I've lost count of how many bounties there are on my head, but it was about a dozen last I checked. It fills me with pride, in a sick sort of way. People out there are scared of me. They better be. Fear is an excellent protection. If people fear you, they're less likely to try and attack you.

I stay in the same crouched position for another few minutes, but when there's still no sound, I get to my feet and take a torch from my backpack. I do a quick sweep of the room. Besides a few dusty cardboard boxes, it's empty, just like I was told. Judging from the thick layer of dust on the floor, nobody has been up here in weeks.

It's quite a pretty space, actually. With a bit of a clean, this would make a lovely attic room. The wooden beams reaching through the floor up to the very top would be perfect to tie a hammock between. So much better than the hole I currently call my home.

A noise down below startles me but my training kicks in enough to keep me from jumping. I stay where I am, feet rooted to the floor, not making a sound. There are footsteps, slow and heavy. More of a shuffling rather than walking. I wasn't told the age of my mark but judging from this sound alone, I'd guess someone old. Those are the easiest. Not just in terms of the job, but also by being easiest on my conscience. Old people die anyway. They don't have much life left for me to steal. Less guilt to live with.

I stay in my position, not daring to do any

movement at all, until the sound of the toilet flushing and more shuffling announce that he's back in his bedroom. Time to act before I get covered in dust like the rest of this room.

Carefully, I move towards the trapdoor. Compared to the rest of the house, it's somewhat modern with shiny metal hinges that look like they won't squeak too much. I work in slow motion, gently opening the trap door and lowering the ladder. The slower I move, the less likely I am to make a sound.

By the time I step off the last rung, I'm bored. I much prefer a quick and easy backstreet assassination over creeping through someone's house. Not only does it take forever, but it also shows me a kind of life that I've never had and never will have. Paintings on the wall. Photographs in dusty frames. A rug frayed at the edges, turned dark by time and too many footsteps. At the end of the corridor is a sorry looking houseplant in a pot too large for it. I bet it's not been watered for weeks. Maybe, once I've killed its owner, I'm going to give it some water. Call it part of the service.

I tiptoe along the hallway towards the sound of gentle snoring. The direction fits with the mental map I've built of the house while I listened to the owner's trip to the toilet. The door on my right will lead to his bedroom. I pull my knives from the scabbards secured to my belt. I only oiled them yesterday, so they don't make a sound as I ready my weapons of choice. Both have been dipped in poison, making this a much subtler method than just stabbing people. A simple nick with my blade and they'll be dead half an hour later. It's more personal than using darts like some of my colleagues. No, let's not call them that. Compatriots. Miserable sods trapped in the same life I am.

I take a deep but soundless breath and push open the door. It's almost completely dark, but my eyes adjust quickly, already used to the dim light from the corridor. There's a figure lying on the bed, covered by several blankets. That man must really be cold. It's late spring and by now, one duvet should suffice.

I carefully approach the bed from the left, my blades at the ready. Maybe I should just use the poison today. Let him drift off into death during his sleep. Much nicer and definitely much less bloody than cutting his throat. His bed sheets are of high quality and I'd hate to ruin them. Maybe he has some heirs who'd like to inherit them without bloodstains.

Putting one of the blades back into its scabbard, I pull a tiny needle from a hidden pocket sewn into the collar of my shirt. Much less impressive than my knives but let's not be too violent today. The carnage I left behind at yesterday's mark made up for that.

I reach over to prick the man - and notice my mistake. The snoring has stopped, and it must have been gone ever since I entered the room. The man in front of me is not breathing.

"Not very bright, are you?"

I whirl around, ready to throw my blade at the man whose voice is coming from a dark corner of the room. A room I hadn't checked for traps. Big mistake. Without taking my eyes off the shadows he's hiding in, I shake the man behind me. He's too light. It's not actually a body. Please tell me I didn't just fall for the pillows-beneath-the-blanket trick. I really deserve to be caught. Too busy getting distracted by pot plants and rugs.

"Who are you?" I challenge him, my voice as sharp as I can make it. Let's not show any insecurity or fear.

"I was told they'd send one of their best," he mutters as if to himself. "I'm not convinced that's you."

"You're my mark?"

He steps out of the shadows and I let my needle drop, pulling my second knife instead. Even in the dim light, it's clear that the man really is old, but that doesn't stop him moving in a strange, fluid way that reminds me of a predator stalking his prey. The shuffling walk to the bathroom must have been an act.

"You took your time," he says instead of an answer. "Although, I guess that's a good sign. Sometimes, patience is more important than intelligence."

He seems intent on insulting me, but I don't react to his provocation. I'm practised in not listening to what other people say to me.

"What do you want?" I ask. Somehow, it's clear to me that he's not here to kill his assassin. He could have done that as soon as I walked through the door. Jumped me from behind, slit my throat or banged a pan against my head. Whatever he fancied.

"I have a proposition for you," he replies calmly. "You're not as good as I expected, but I suppose you'll have to do. How would you like to become self-employed?"

I chuckle humourlessly. "No chance in hell."

Not because I don't want to, but because I can't. I'm

not going to tell him that. Never give away your weaknesses.

"Because of the collar around your neck?" he asks.

My mind takes a stumble. How did he know? Nobody does. Instinctively, my hand flies to my throat, checking if my scarf is still in place. It is. He shouldn't be able to see the collar.

"How?" I ask, knowing that he'll know exactly what I mean.

He chuckles. "Trade secret. But here's the deal. I remove the collar, you start your own agency. I'll occasionally give you marks, but otherwise, you're independent. I might even throw in a cash injection to start you off."

I want to gape and throw a thousand questions at him, but I keep my expression neutral. "What do you get out of it?"

He laughs again. "I've been wanting to leave this city for a while. Let's pretend you killed me. I get peace and quiet, you can have the house and my existing contact lists. That should help you get things running."

Confusion is slowing my brain down. He wants me to start my own assassin business? Take my collar? Give me his house? This has to be a test.

"Prove it," I challenge him. "Prove you can get rid of this thing."

I rip my scarf off my neck, exposing the bronze collar around my throat. I've grown used to the tightness of it, the way it's almost painful when I swallow. The few times when I was without one, back when I was still growing and needed to be fitted a new one every year or so, I felt almost naked without it. It's become part of me, part of my identity. We all have them. Everyone in the Pack.

"I'll need to come closer," he warns me. "And what do you think about some light?"

He flicks the light switch before I can say something and the lamp above me flickers on. It's a dim, energy saving one that will take a moment to get to full brightness. I'm glad, it makes it easier on my eyes.

Finally, I get to see my mark. He's surprisingly tall with a black top hat on his white hair. A well-manicured beard hides his angular chin, but it doesn't distract from the deep scars lining both of his cheekbones. If they weren't there, he'd look like a gentleman, an academic perhaps who spends most of his life behind a desk or surrounded by books. Those scars though tell a different story.

"Who are you?" I ask, repeating my question before a suspicion makes its way through my confusion. "Did you put a mark on yourself to get me here?"

"Good," is all he says as he walks towards me. I fight my instincts to flinch and run away, staying rooted in my spot instead. I'm too curious for my own good. Letting someone as dangerous as him close to me is never a good idea. But here I am, unmoving as he lifts his right hand to my neck while his left disappears in his jacket pocket.

Curiosity killed the cat. They'd put that on my gravestone if anyone bothered to bury me. Which is unlikely. I'll probably end up a corpse floating in a river or thrown into one of those big communal rubbish bins.

A fitting end to a life that's consisted of not much else besides killing and thieving.

I pull the collar of my shirt out of the way as he gently runs his fingers over the collar.

"They've progressed a bit since I last saw them, but it's simple enough. Don't move, this won't take long."

He closes his eyes. This would be the perfect moment to take him out. Do what I'm supposed to do and return home, pick up breakfast and then nap for a bit.

But no, I'm stupid and curious. If there's a chance he can rid me of the collar that's determined my life until this very point, it's worth the risk. People before me have tried to take off the collars. All of them have failed. I don't know why I even believe this man. It's likely just a trick. I already fell for his illusions once. The first time was an accident, a moment of absentmindedness, the second is plain stupidity and recklessness.

Well, I never said I was clever.

"It's going to open in a moment," the man mutters. "Steel yourself, this may be overwhelming."

He doesn't give me any time to prepare. The collar springs open with a strange crunching sound and I suck in a deep breath, staggering back. My heartbeat is growing faster, and I can feel the hairs on my skin stand up. A growl comes from my throat.

"Easy there," the man says soothingly. "You can keep control. You're strong."

Tears prick my eyes when pain shoots through my fingertips. I don't need to look down to know that my claws have just broken through my skin. I blink rapidly, the colours of the room changing whenever I blink, alternating between the bright room and blurry, washed out shapes. Like a painter ran a sponge over his artwork to soak up parts of the colours and the clear lines.

"You're in control."

My ears flick towards the man's voice. He's louder now and I can hear nuances in his tone that weren't there before.

Memories flood my mind. I've experienced this before. Long ago. Before the collar was fixed around my neck. Running through long grass, so many scents, the sounds of insects as loud as traffic noise. My paws soft on the ground, my claws...

Control. I take another deep breath and focus on that thought. Control. I'm in control. Not the animal. Not the beast hiding inside of me.

Slowly, the claws retreat and my heartbeat slows down. It takes another minute for my vision to go back to normal, but I don't take my eyes off the old man who's retreated back to the corner, watching me.

"They chose well, sending you here tonight," he says when I'm ready. "You've got enough control to deal with it. You wouldn't have needed a collar. They should have taken it off ages ago. Well, their loss is my gain. But let's talk business."

"Business?" I ask, my mouth dry. I feel strange. Like that weakness you get just before you fall ill, where you don't quite know what's going on and you can't put your finger on why you're not feeling as well as you usually do. I run my hand over my throat. The skin where the collar sat is soft and sensitive. Weak. I flip up the collar of my shirt and put my scarf back on. And remember that I should probably warn the man.

"You may want to take this," I say and throw a tiny vial towards him that I had hidden in one of the many pockets of my shirt.

He catches it easily and looks at it curiously. "What's that?"

"Antidote to the poison I gave you." I grin. "Sorry, I wasn't sure if you'd actually take off the collar or had some more sinister plans."

He raises an eyebrow. "Darts?"

I nod. "Hidden in my collar. I pricked you when you put your hands around my throat."

"Well, I didn't see that coming. Impressive. Seems you're cleverer than you look."

He uncorks the vial and swallows the contents. I'm amazed he trusts me not to poison him. Of course, I've already done that, but it could always be a double bluff.

He screws up his face at the taste. "Next time, add a little cinnamon. It enhances the aftertaste."

I keep my face passive. "I'll keep it under advisement."

"There's a lab in the basement. In the office, you'll find a folder with all the necessary key codes to get around the house and into the important rooms."

He picks up on my questioning look.

"The weapons storage, the lab I mentioned, the training gym and the morgue."

This time, I can't help but gasp. "A morgue? In this house?"

He looks at me strangely.

"Of course. Doesn't your current employer have one?"

I shake my head. "We just dispose of the bodies or leave them to be found."

He clucks his tongue. "Such a waste. There is much to learn about death by studying corpses. And you never know when you might need a well-placed corpse to send someone a message."

In a way, he makes sense, but at the same time, do I want to live in a house above a morgue? Then I remind myself: I'm an assassin. The one thing I'm really not scared about is death. There are a lot worse things on Earth than death itself.

"I don't think my current employer," I emphasise that last word as it's the one thing I'd never call Brut, "will just let me go. He's invested in me, he's trained me. He won't accept me leaving and opening my own agency."

"Don't worry about that," the man says dismissively. "He won't trouble you. What you need to concern yourself with is who to hire. I have a lot of work for you and you won't be able to handle it all on your own. You can start small, but at some point, I expect you to have at least as many employees as your current manager."

Employer, manager, is he using euphemisms or does he really believe that's how it works? Slavemaster would be more accurate. Owner. It's not like we ever signed up to work for him. There's no wage either. Does this man expect me to be like Brut or does he want me to run things differently?

"You'll find everything else you need in the office,

including your first case. Of course, you're free to do as you wish, but my only condition is that my assignments always take priority over others. In return, you get the house, some cash and, of course, a collarless life. Do you agree?"

I don't have to think twice. Not because I wholeheartedly agree with all he's promising. I'm expecting him to break his promises anyway. But no, I'm good at double-crossing people. Very good. And no matter what he believes of me, the one thing I'm really good at is looking out for myself.

CHAPTER ONE

6 MONTHS LATER

He smells of sweat and fear. I cross my legs, the heels of my feet on the desk I'm currently sitting behind. Although lounging would be a better term. Mud is dripping from the soles of my boots. I'll have to clean that up later, but it works well for the badass appearance I'm trying to exude. I'm not someone to mess with. I don't care about rules, conventions and dress codes. While the man on the other side of the desk is wearing a pristine suit, I'm in my usual leather tights and tunic. Tights because they don't get in the way when fighting or jumping off buildings, and a tunic because it's longer than a shirt and therefore has more space for hidden pockets. All in black, of course. Blood stains are a pain to get out of clothes. I'm nothing but practical.

My hair is hidden beneath the black cap I've started wearing recently. I think it makes me look more mysterious, although Lily keeps telling me to take it off.

That girl has no sense for making an outfit convey a message. A dangerous one, in this case. Don't mess with me, that's what my clothes are saying. Especially the muddy boots on my desk.

The man clears his throat.

"You came highly recommended," he mutters as if he's not quite sure if he's allowed to speak.

I raise an eyebrow. "Who recommended me?"

His eyes widen. Typical deer in headlights look. He's scared but not just of me.

"Contacts," he says evasively. "I'm willing to pay whatever fee you charge."

Immediately, my price list increases by about ten times what I'd usually tell him. I do like wealthy customers. They rarely care what I charge other people who are less well-off.

"What is it that you need from me?" I ask, studying him closely. He doesn't look like a man who's used to dealing with assassins. He's an office kind of guy who only ever reads about shady things in the newspaper.

"My brother was killed. I need you to find whoever did it."

That makes me sit up a little straighter. "You've come to the wrong place, sir," I say with a trace of condescension. "I don't find killers. I send them."

He cringes visibly. "Once you've found whoever killed my brother, you're welcome to kill the bastard."

I purse my lips. This is unusual. Actually, this has never happened before. I've done this job for half a year now, very successfully, but nobody has ever asked me to find an assassin.

"What if one of my people killed your brother?" I ask, taking my feet off the desk to look at my records. "What's his name?"

"I don't think it was a professional," he mutters, not looking me in the eye. "It seemed unplanned and very violent." He shudders slightly. "There was a lot of blood."

Interesting. He's right, that doesn't sound like an assassin did it. We take pride in leaving a crime scene as neat as possible. Don't want to make it too easy for the police.

"What's his name?" I repeat.

"Winston Kindler. 14B Merchant Street. He had a sweet shop there."

Sweets? Maybe I need to take on this case myself. It sounds enticing.

I flick through my box of index cards, but I already know that I won't find a Mr Kindler in there. While I don't do all the jobs myself, I deal with all our clients. I remember the names of our marks.

"What are the police doing?" I ask absentmindedly.

"Nothing," he says, anger lacing his voice. "They're convinced it was a mugging, but his wallet wasn't taken. The cash register was emptied, but the safe was intact. It was early in the day, so there wouldn't have been much in the money box anyway. It doesn't make sense."

I nod. "Let's pretend I was to take this case. What kind of remuneration are we talking about?"

For the first time since he entered my office, he smiles.

"How about a blank cheque?"

🐾 🐾 🐾 🐾 🐾 🐾

THERE'S A HEAD IN THE FRIDGE. I SIGH. NOT AGAIN.

"Lily!" I shout. "I told you, no body parts in the kitchen!"

My friend laughs. "Until you fix the morgue's cooling chamber, the fridge is the only place to keep them."

I groan. We've had a problem with that cooling room for two months now. Whenever I think it's fixed, it stops working again. It's like the basement is haunted.

"I'll get on it," I promise. "We just got a very rich new client, so I'll be able to afford a professional handyman this time."

Not Jock from around the corner who did it for free in the hope for a kiss from Lily. I think he made it worse. And didn't get a kiss, obviously. Lily isn't into guys although she doesn't usually tell them. She likes to use her looks to her advantage.

I close the fridge, unwilling to stare into the dead woman's eyes for much longer. To be fair, one of her eyes is missing, but while it's not enough to put me off my dinner, it's also not very appetising.

"Get a second fridge for now," I tell Lily. "I think you need it often enough to warrant the cost."

She grins widely. She likes to play with her prey when she gets the chance. Sometimes, that involves taking random body parts home to later send them to her marks' families. That may sound evil, but actually, Lily is a really nice girl. She just has a bit of a violent streak.

"What's for dinner?" I ask, now that I know that there's nothing edible in the fridge.

"Robbie was going to bring home some takeaway," she says with a shrug. "He's not home yet though, so we may have to wait for a bit longer. Hungry?"

I nod. "Could eat a dinosaur."

She laughs. "I don't think they're on the menu. Let's see what's left in the living room. I think there was half a bag of crisps left last night."

I don't meet her gaze. "Not anymore."

Lily puts her hands on her hips and glares at me. "Glutton."

I shrug. "They were there. I'm an assassin, I kill things. Even if it's just crisps. They're basically dead potatoes."

She chuckles. "So, what's this new rich client about? The one who's financing our new cooling chamber?"

I follow her into the living room, where she magically produces a bar of chocolate and a handful of dried peanuts. They look drier than they should, so I stick with the chocolate for now.

We throw ourselves onto the biggest sofa. It's not my furniture, at least I didn't buy any of it. It came with the house. I've been planning to get something more to my taste at some point, but money's been tight. When the mysterious man offered me a 'cash injection' to start my business off with, he was talking about a rather small syringe, and I used most of that to pay off the Pack. I shouldn't complain though. I've got a house, an office, even a morgue. I had none of that before. And I even got rid of my collar. Win-win.

"He wants me to find whoever killed his brother," I say with a certain distaste.

"Wait, that's new." Lily laughs. "So… you're not going to kill anyone?"

I shrug. "I've got permission to kill the killer, if I find them."

"That's weird. Why would he come to you?"

"No idea. Maybe the Pack refused his request. Maybe he only knows about me and not about any of the others in town. I have no clue, but the pay is totally worth the confusion."

She raises an eyebrow. "How much?"

I give her a cheeky wink. "Enough. We'll be able to fix the house, pay ourselves some nice salaries and feed a few stray cats at the same time."

Lily chuckles. "You need to stop feeding them. I had two kittens sitting on the doorstep this morning, begging for food. I think they're beginning to learn to come here if they're hungry. That's all your fault."

"Can't help it," I shrug. "It's in my nature to help my fellow felines."

She grins. "I'm not a feline, and yet you helped me."

I sigh. "Okay, and friends. Felines and non-feline friends. Better?"

"Much. How are you going to find the killer, though? You don't have any experience with solving murders."

"I'm sure I'm going to come up with something. First of all, I'm going to inspect the crime scene, then find some witnesses. That's how they do it in books."

She laughs again. "You're going to crack this case, I'm sure. Let me know if you need my help, although

I'm quite busy with my current mark. He's such a bore, but he loves his new girlfriend." She chuckles. "Pity she's not actually real."

Lily grins widely. She's a predator playing with her prey before killing it. She loves to make men go crazy for her, then kills them right when they realise that they've been fooled. Break their hearts before stabbing them. She's evil in a fun way. Just like all of us. The Pride, my team of outcast assassins and ragtag thieves. So far, there are only five of us, but we've already managed to make a name for ourselves. Our reputation is increasing with every kill, and we're very efficient at killing. I still can't believe that six months ago, I was a slave, working for the Pack because they had me collared. Now, I'm my own woman. A businesswoman. I work for myself, pay myself, even employ other people. And not a single one of them is collared. They're all here because they want to be.

I yawn, tiredness catching up with me. I was up late last night, running over the roofs of the town, checking out the location of an assassination we're planning. I'm likely going to pass it on to one of the others now that I have a more lucrative job. This strange murder case is getting priority. We need the money.

"I'll head to bed," I announce. It takes all my stomach muscles to get up from the sofa. It's far too low and soft. Once I solve the murder, I'm going to buy us a new one.

"Sweet dreams," Lily says with a cheeky smile. "I might head out and have some fun."

I leave her to it and climb up the stairs until I reach

the ladder leading up to the attic. I smile when I remember how I first came here. Back then, I thought what a lovely home this would make. How the loft would be perfect as a bedroom. Now, it's become exactly that.

I climb the ladder and pull it up behind me, closing the trapdoor. I like my privacy. In the past few months, I've transformed the room into my own personal sanctum. Large pillows are strewn all over the floor that's now covered in dozens of rugs. A few shelves are clinging to the sloping ceiling, but the best part about the room is the hammock, strung between two of the large wooden beams. I quickly change into something more comfortable and check that the window is closed properly. I broke in through it once, and I know how easy it would be for others to do just the same. I've had it reglazed with very thick glass though. It should be strong enough to withstand anyone kicking against it.

There's a small sound from outside that has me open the window to check it out.

Someone is meowing softly. I lean out of the window until I see the tiny kitten clinging to the top of the window frame. It must have been running over the roofs but then got stuck on top of the dormer window. Poor thing. I stretch out a hand and begin to purr. I don't want it to scratch me.

Its ears flick when it realises that I'm making the soothing sound. It's probably confused by a human sounding like a cat. They always are.

Slowly, it steps onto my hand, just about fitting on it.

I gently carry it into the room and put it onto the floor. It stares at me with large yellow eyes.

"Now what?" I ask. "I'm not going to take you all the way downstairs. You'll have to sleep here tonight."

The kitten hisses. I know it understands me.

"Sorry," I tell it. "I'm tired. It's not my fault you got stuck."

Not wanting to be completely selfish, I pour some water from a bottle into a bowl and put it on the floor. At least the kitten will have something to drink.

"Now it's time to sleep," I yawn. I climb onto my hammock and am instantly transported into the land of dreams.

CHAPTER TWO

M*eow. Meow.*
I blink open my eyes only to stare into big yellow pupils lined with black. Whiskers stroke my cheeks.

I groan and close my eyes again. It feels way too early.

Meow.

"Shut up," I mutter and hide my head beneath a pillow.

In response, the kitten begins to claw my shirt. Great. An alarm clock with claws. Worst invention ever.

"Piss off," I growl, but the cat doesn't budge. It's probably hungry.

I breathe in deep. It's a male. Usually, I don't let males into my bed. I sleep with them in theirs and leave before sunrise. That's the rule. No attachments. Luckily, this little male isn't human.

Meooooow.

"Okay then," I sigh dramatically and sit up,

surprising the kitten. He tumbles and lands on my thighs, meowing indignantly.

I don't apologise. It's his fault for standing on my chest.

Yawning loudly, I pick him up and climb out of the hammock. Usually, I'd get dressed, but the kitten won't stop asking for food. I'm far too easily manipulated.

I take him downstairs into the kitchen. The house is quiet, I seem to be the first one awake.

"Don't look," I warn him and open one of the cabinets, revealing my stash of cat food. It's my guilty little secret. Even to me, it smells appetising, but I've got enough of a grip on my feral side to resist the temptation. I put some of the food in a bowl and hand it to the kitten. He starts eating greedily, leaving me with an amused smile on my face.

While he's enjoying his breakfast, I make myself some beans on toast. It's that kind of day. In a way, the beans almost look like wet cat food. Not sure if that makes them more or less enticing.

Meow.

He's already finished his food and still sounds hungry. Cats. Greedy little bastards.

I grin and give him some more. I feel like giving him a name, but he probably already has one. To find out, I'd need to shift, but I'm not in the mood. I know cats can understand me when I'm human, but I only understand the intentions behind their meows, not actual words like names.

Maybe I'll shift later, although by then, he'll likely be gone. Unless what Lily said is true and I am training the local cats to come here for food. I can't help it.

Suddenly, a thought strikes my mind and I almost meow myself. I think I've just had the most brilliant idea.

I crouch down so I'm closer to the little kitten. He ignores me, busy eating the last remaining crumbs. No idea how he's managed to devour two bowls of cat food this fast. Even I would have taken longer than that.

"Hey little one," I say quietly. "Shall we make a deal?"

His ears twitch, but he continues eating.

"How about I give you food every day, and in return, you run some errands for me? Go to places and check them out? Tell me if there are any humans around? Stuff like that?"

I can feel how he's thinking about it, but he's too distracted by his meal. I sigh and wait for him to finish.

He rubs his face with his front paws, and I think my heart is close to melting. He's too cute for my cold assassin heart. Maybe I shouldn't get involved with baby cats. They're bound to change me into a bubbling mess.

"So, what do you say?" I ask again. "Want to spy for me?"

Even though I'm not shifted, I feel his assent and grin. I've won a spy that nobody will ever suspect. Granted, he won't be able to tell me what the humans he sees are talking about, but he'll be able to do some reconnaissance. Cats are everywhere, and most people don't pay much attention to them. Very few people know that I can talk to them. This is going to be epic.

I pick up the kitten and carry him to the front door.

"Come again tomorrow, and I'll give you both food and a mission."

He looks at me with eyes so intelligent that I don't have any doubts about the success of this new venture.

An image of other cats pops into my mind.

I smile. "Yes, you can bring your friends too, if they're interested."

He turns around and runs off, not giving me a second glance. Cats usually give me more attention than they give humans, but they still don't like to appear needy or tamed. They always keep their word though. Cats may be devious at times, but they're honest about it.

I go back inside and eat my own breakfast. The beans have turned cold and the toast soggy, but I don't mind. In my head, I'm already making plans for an underground cat network. I'll have to order more cat food. Lily won't like it, but she'll see the advantage of it soon enough. I know disliking cats is intrinsic to her nature, but she's come to like me. I'm her best friend and vice versa.

I yawn and put my plate in the sink, hoping that someone will clean it. The probability of that is tiny, but that doesn't stop me. I have more important things to deal with than dirty dishes.

In my office, I put my feet on the desk as always and take the top folder from my entry tray. Inside, a photograph of the murder victim stares at me. The man is still alive in the picture, but his eyes have a strange haunted, terrified look. He was either anxious in general or scared of whoever took the photo. I draw a little question mark next to the picture. It's as good a starting point as any.

The victim's brother has written a short statement on the next page. According to him, Winston Kindler was a quiet, reclusive man with very few hobbies. He went fishing occasionally, but not much else. No drug habits, no alcohol addiction. No mention of gambling either. A man so dull that even reading his file makes me yawn. All Winston seemed to do was work in his sweet shop and sit at home. Guess his shop is where I need to head to first.

So far, there are no reasons at all for why someone would want to kill him.

I take a notepad and scribble some instructions for Benjamin: *Bank accounts, police records, medical information.*

Benjamin is a thief, the best, and he'll easily get me that info. No need to actually ask people for those documents. It's much quicker to just steal them. Maybe I'll see some new lines of enquiry once he's got them for me, but for now, I'm stuck with taking a look at the crime scene and the shop. Doesn't sound terribly exciting. Definitely not as fun as a good assassination. Then I remember that glorious blank cheque and decide that visiting a sweet shop will be a lovely thing to do.

WINSTON KINDLER'S SHOP ISN'T CLOSED LIKE I expected. No, there's a queue of children snaking all the way around the street corner. Most of them are waiting patiently in line, but others are jumping up and down excitedly. What the fuck is going on? Also, is there no school today? Sometimes, I lose track, but I'm pretty sure it's not a weekend today.

I choose a girl who's standing by her own, looking a little lost.

"What's going on?" I ask her, nodding towards the shop.

She smiles shyly. "They're giving away free sweets."

I raise my eyebrows. "Are they? Do you know why?"

She nods. "The owner died, and he said in his will that all the sweets should be given away for free."

The girl grins, exposing some blackened teeth. I'm tempted to tell her that she shouldn't eat any more sweets but then ignore that thought. She wouldn't listen to me anyway.

I let her be and walk to the entrance of the shop. Some of the children grumble about me skipping the queue, but nobody actually confronts me. I'm trying to keep my usual talk-to-me-and-I'll-kill-you aura to a minimum, but it's hard to let go of that habit. The fewer people know me, the fewer can testify against me in court. Or kill me.

I squeeze past a few rowdy boys until I'm inside the shop. It's every child's dream. Large glass jars full of sweets in every single colour are packed onto shelves that seem to cover every inch of available space. It smells like chocolate and liquorice, making me forget that I've already had breakfast.

A young woman stands behind the counter, weighing sweets on antique brass scales. I wait until she's poured them in a paper bag and handed them to one of the boys before approaching her. The children behind me complain quietly as I interrupt the queue.

"It's for children only, madam," the girl says. She's barely out of childhood herself, maybe seventeen at most. Her apron is full of sugar dust and syrup stains. She's rather plain, but her eyes sparkle with intelligence.

"I'm not here for the sweets," I say, working hard to keep the regret from my voice. I really hope she's going to offer me some mints despite my words. "I'm here about the owner, Mr Kindler."

"Such a tragedy," she mutters. "He was so kind to everyone. I don't know why anyone would want to kill him."

"You're aware he was murdered?" I ask, a little surprised.

She nods. "Oh yes, we're neighbours. I saw his body." She shudders. "It wasn't a pretty sight. But let's not talk about that in front of the children."

Her eyes flick to the boys behind us who are listening with wide eyes. This is going to be the gossip in all of the town's schoolyards soon.

"I agree. Do you have a break soon?"

She looks at her watch, a heavy, expensive one. Strange for a shop girl to wear one like that. An heirloom, maybe?"

"Officially in one hour, but with all that's going on, it might take longer. The news is spreading fast, and I think every single child in the city is on their way here. I wouldn't be surprised if I'll be standing behind the counter all day or until the sweets are gone. It was a lovely gesture of Win... Mr Kindler to do this, but it's hard work for me."

For a split second, a shadow darkens her expression, as if she's not impressed with her former employer. I file it away in my mind, along with her almost calling him by his first name.

Grudgingly, I nod. "I'll be back in the evening. Here's my card in case you're done before I get here."

I'm really glad I had those business cards printed. It doesn't say much on them, only my address and a phone number. No mention of assassinations. That would be tasteless.

"Meow?" she asks, frowning.

"My business name," I reply. "It's an acronym."

I don't tell her what it stands for because I don't know myself. Ever since I came up with the silly name, I've been trying to find an explanation that I can give to clients, something to pretend that it wasn't just a dumb joke. I never thought this whole business thing would actually take off. I would have chosen a slightly more serious name otherwise. But for now, I'm stuck with Meow. Masters in Ending Others... Whatever.

She slides my card into the front pocket of her apron, then gives me an annoyed look as if she's wondering why I'm still here, stopping the masses of children behind me from getting their sweets.

"See you later," I tell her, making it sound more like a threat than a promise. I'm not used to being nice to people. The people I deal with usually end up dead anyway, so there's no reason to waste time and emotional energy on pretending to like them. I can be professional with my clients, but I'm sure none of them would describe me as 'nice'. Pleasantly cool, perhaps. Frosty helpful. But as long as they pay my fees, I don't care what they think. They don't matter to me in the slightest.

I leave the sweet shop, almost wishing that I'd got myself a bag of mints. The smell in there has made me hungry. Breakfast feels too long ago. My metabolism has been crazy recently. I eat three times as much as I used to. Maybe it's the fact that I now have money to buy as much food as I want, or perhaps it's the effect of no longer wearing a collar. It's a little annoying, having to spend time on getting or making food several times a day, but at the same time, I've realised how much I like food. The little kick I get from of a well-arranged platter, the tastes of a new dish, the tingle of the spices I've discovered in the corner of the weekly market. Food is no longer just sustenance for me, it's become a hobby.

Maybe it's a good thing that my current case is partly set in a sweet shop. I'll have an excuse to return there and perhaps sample the contents of those big glasses. For research purposes, obviously.

CHAPTER THREE

For now, I ignore the twinge of hunger poking my stomach and head towards the dead man's house. It's not far from the shop, just a few streets away. He had an easy commute to work. I'm almost jealous.

It's a pretty but boring neighbourhood. Neat little terraced houses, most of their gardens expertly manicured. I gag at the thought of someone actually sitting there, making sure every bit of grass is as tall as the rest. How quaint.

Mr Kindler's house is one of five identical ones squeezed into one large unsightly block. It's like someone took a handful of dough and cut it into five thin slices, not caring that they might be too small to live in. I know that Mr Kindler lived alone and I doubt there would have been space for more than just one person in this tiny house-slice.

I give the street another once over. No one is around, no curtains are moving to suggest curious onlookers. It seems everyone's at work, school or whatever else ordinary people do at eleven in the morning. Fishing, maybe. Who knows. I've never been among normal people. I usually just kill them.

Confident that nobody is watching me, I head up the tiny driveway – barely large enough to allow a bike to be parked there – and fish a key from my pocket. There's no sign of any police activity. No police tape, no stickers warning me not to enter. They must have decided that there's no evidence worth protecting in the house. Let's see if I'll come to other conclusions. It wouldn't be the first time for me to outthink the police.

The door opens with a squeak. It could do with some oil. Maybe he left it like that intentionally as a sort of alarm bell. But somehow I doubt he was thinking in those sort of ways. The only indication I have of him being anything but the boring man his brother has described him as is that mugshot with haunted eyes and a slightly scared expression. It's not much to go on. I might be reading too much into that picture, but my instincts rarely prove me wrong.

There's a short hallway ending in carpeted stairs at the end. Two doors lead to either side, and I decide to check out the kitchen to my right. It's small, not that I expected anything else. It's also incredibly tidy. So clean that I doubt he's cooked in here. I randomly open some of the cupboards. Most of them are empty; the others sport a few basics like rice and sugar. His fridge contains nothing but a single can of cider and a piece of cheese that looks like it's seen healthier days. Again, it doesn't look like Mr Kindler made much use of the kitchen.

After opening even more drawers and cupboards

and finding nothing, I head over to the living room opposite the kitchen. A worn sofa and a tv on a stained wooden cabinet is the only furniture. No bookshelves, no floor lamps, not even a rug. There's not a single cushion on the sofa. Who the heck doesn't have pillows?

I take the remote control from the cabinet and press a few random buttons. Nothing happens. I check the socket, but there doesn't seem to be power. Great. A living room with nothing to do other than a tv which isn't even working. Mr Kindler must have been incredibly boring. Or not who everyone thinks he was.

I throw the remote on the sofa – and pick it up again. There's something strange about it, something I didn't realise before. It's the wrong weight. It's too light. I turn it around and open the cover hiding the battery compartment. It's empty. Why aren't there batteries in the remote control? Sure, you don't really need it if the tv isn't working, but why bother removing the batteries when you could just leave them in?

Slowly, I run my fingers over the black plastic. It still feels wrong. I close my eyes, focusing on my sense of touch. Optics can lie, but touch usually doesn't. There's something beneath the bottom of the battery compartment. Like… a second layer. How clever. I pry it open with my fingernails, revealing a key stuck in a small space underneath. It's a nondescript metal key that could open anything. I extract it and slip it into my pocket. Hopefully, I'll find the matching lock soon. This case is beginning to be a little more interesting.

Now that I know that not everything in this house may be as it seems, I continue my exploration with a little more excitement. There's nothing else in the living room, but when I turn over the drawer of the bedroom cabinet, I grin. Bingo. There's an envelope taped to the bottom of it. I'm kind of disappointed when there's nothing but money in there, but when I count it, I revise my opinion. That's a *lot* of money for a sweet shop owner. Hell, it's more than my mysterious benefactor gave me. With this, I could fix up the house *and* give us all a holiday. I'm glad nobody is around to see my devious smile. I'm trained to keep my expression neutral, but it's tough to keep a straight face when you're looking at over a thousand darems. I slip it into a pocket hidden in the lining of my coat and put the drawer back in place. Finders, keepers.

What I really want to find is whatever the key opens. A safe? A hidden drawer? A door to a secret room? Sadly, there's not a single locked keyhole in the entire house. That's strange in itself. Even in his little office, none of the drawers is locked. In one, I find some more money, but compared to the banknotes hidden in his bedroom, this is peanuts. This amount fits the image of the sweet shop owner I had in my mind. Enough to pay expenses and maybe an unplanned repair, but nothing that could provoke suspicion. That's what the entire house feels like. Average, bending to stereotypes, everything *exactly* like what you'd expect. That in itself makes me want to discover something incriminating. Nobody is this boring. Especially not someone who got murdered.

There are some random bills and invoices in his desk drawers. The sight of them makes me yawn. I have the same waiting for me in my in-tray in my own office. I like to ignore them. They give me a headache. It seems Mr Kindler did the same. Some of these bills are from last year, and they don't look like he ever even took them out of the drawer.

After one final sweep of his house, I head out into his perfectly manicured back garden. It's basically just a small stretch of grass leading to the tiniest garden shed I've ever seen. It's too low for me to enter without bending my head and I'm not the tallest woman around. Inside are a lawn mower and some other tools that I wouldn't even know what to do with. I've never had a garden, and I'm not planning to have one in the future. I'm not a garden person.

I can picture Winston Kindler here though. Kneeling on a foam mat, using scissors to cut his grass into the perfect length. Boring. I've tried having plants in the house to make it look more like a home, but they usually die. Mostly because I kill them. Old habits die hard. Kat, the plant assassin. Yup, that's me. Yet another title to add to my business card. It might be easier to explain than Meow.

Something about this shed irritates me, and I throw all the tools outside until the hut is empty. Sadly, there's no hidden cache. Not even a trap door. I do love a pretty trap door, but they're hard to come by nowadays.

Disappointed, I put everything back inside, not really caring that it now looks like an earthquake made everything fall from shelves and hooks. The lawn mower is last. It's bright red and reminds me of a ladybug for some reason. When I lift it to put it back in the shed, something on the cord catches my eye. There are numbers scribbled on the orange rubber.

3 9 5 7 2 0 4

It's not printed on the cord; otherwise I'd assume it would be a barcode or something like that. No, it's drawn there in shaky, uneven marker pen. I write the numbers in my little notebook, kind of hoping that they're the combination for a safe or something exciting like that. With my luck, it might just be his favourite numbers that he's written there because he was bored with being a boring sweet shop owner.

I sigh. I now have a key and a series of numbers but don't know what to do with them. I've explored the entire house and the garden – not that there's a lot to explore here besides the shed – but found nothing of interest. Except for the fact that it doesn't look very lived in. No cushions on the sofa, an empty fridge, brand new bedding and even the tools in the shed look unused. It's like Winston Kindler lived somewhere else and only used this as a pretend home. But why would anyone do that? It doesn't make any sense. Maybe I'll find more answers in the sweet shop.

CHAPTER FOUR

I grab a sandwich on the way, knowing that the sweet shop will make me hungry again. I don't see how anyone can work there without being fat as a dog. I'd probably get fired on my first day for eating too much. Maybe it's because I never got any sweets while growing up. Now that I can decide what I eat and when, sugar plays a major part in my diet.

There are still children waiting in front of the shop, but the queue has grown a lot shorter. I ignore them and head inside, impatient to wait even longer. The girl is still behind the counter, now looking decidedly exhausted. No wonder, if she's been handing out sweets all day. At least I got to explore the neighbourhood.

When she sees me, she sighs. "I'm still not done."

"Is there a back room I can wait in?" I ask her, and she sighs again.

"There's a small office. Don't touch anything, I'll be with you as soon as possible."

I smile pleasantly and let her guide me into the office

which is just off the shoproom. She didn't exaggerate when she called it small. It's basically just a desk, a shelf and an old leather chair that looks like it's about to fall apart. The shelf is brimming with folders and papers. Completely the opposite with Mr Kindler's home office. This room actually looks like it's been used regularly. The desk is cluttered with letters and bills.

The girl has returned to the shop and I can hear her talking to the kids, so nothing is stopping me from exploring. Did she mention something about not touching anything? No, I don't think so. It must have been deleted from my memory.

The documents on the desk are boring. Electricity bills, train tickets, invoices for large amounts of sweets. Nothing unusual in the slightest. I make my way through the two drawers. They're stacked to the top with more sheets of paper. There's no order to it, no filing system at all. It's like he simply threw everything into a drawer and hoped that it would sort itself. In a way, I find that endearing, but it makes my job a lot harder.

The bottom drawer is a very different beast. It only contains a small metal lockbox. The shop's earnings, perhaps? There's no key and sadly, the keyhole is too small for the key I found at Winston Kindler's home.

I rattle the box. The sound of coins rattling against the metal confirms my suspicions. There's definitely money in there. Maybe the girl has the key.

Disappointed by the lack of anything exciting or discriminating, I turn to the shelf behind me. I can't help but sigh. This is chaos. Folders of all shapes and sizes, a few tattered books and stacks of old papers. How is anyone supposed to find something in that mess?

I randomly take a blue folder and leaf through its pages. Inventories from ten years ago. Seriously? Why would Mr Kindler need to know how many mints and how many caramel delights he had ten years ago? Maybe he never got around going through his files. Perhaps he was emotionally attached to the inventories. Who knows. I don't really care.

The next few files I look at are just as dull. I think I better stick to killing people.

The girl rescues me from boredom. When I hear her close the shop door, I quickly put the files back to where I found them. More or less. Nobody would notice in this chaos anyway.

I cross my legs and try to appear innocent. She stops in front of the desk and gives me a suspicious look.

"Did you touch anything?" she asks me with a frown.

I hold up my hands. "You told me not to."

"That's not what I asked," she sighs, but then lets herself fall onto the second chair in the room, her exhaustion evident. No wonder, she's been dealing with greedy children all day.

"It must be hard, all by yourself," I say, pretending to be a nice person. I've heard that sometimes, that can have a better result than threatening. Let's see. I'm not quite convinced yet.

She shrugs. "It will be over soon. Now that most of the sweets are gone, I'm going to try and get rid of the rest and then the shop will be sold. I'll have to look for a new job."

She looks defeated, her earlier spunk gone.

"Did he leave you nothing?" I ask gently. "Was it his wish for the shop to be sold?"

She nods. "He'd planned to sell the shop next year anyway. He never told me why because business was going well. The kids loved him. Granted, that was mainly because of his low prices and not because he was particularly good with children, but still. They kept coming back and spent their pocket money in our shop." She quickly corrects herself. "In his shop."

I pity the girl. I'd almost be tempted to offer her a job, but I don't think she's cut out to be in my line of work.

"What's your name?" I ask her, realising that I never actually did. Yes, I know, my people skills suck.

"Caitlin," she replies with a smile. "Caitlin Baumann. You never told me yours."

I smile back and ignore the question. "Tell me about Mr Kindler. How was he as an employer?"

She shrugs. "He always paid me on time. He never got angry or shouty. He expected me to do my job well, but he could be understanding if I needed a day off to help look after my little brothers."

"Did he have any money trouble?"

Caitlin shakes her head. "No, I don't think so. If he did, he never mentioned it. As I said, he always paid my salary, and I earned more here than in my previous jobs. I liked working for him."

Boring. Boring. Boring. I have to remind me of the pay cheque that is waiting for me. Otherwise I'd run out screaming. I'm not made to be an investigator. I'm much better at killing. It doesn't involve actually having to talk to people and pretending to care about their answers.

I sigh. "There must be something that would make people want to kill him."

She shakes her head again. "I can't think of anything and believe me, I've tried finding a reason why he was murdered. He didn't talk about his personal life, but I always had the impression that he was quite a happy man without many worries. If he did, he hid them well."

Now it's my turn to sigh. "So, you have no idea why this happened?"

"No, I don't. It's as much a mystery to me as it is to you," she snaps. "But his death destroyed any chances of me having a stable job and income, so I'm not pleased about it. I certainly wouldn't have wanted him dead, if that's what you're going to ask next."

I lean back in the uncomfortable office chair, desperately wishing I was somewhere else. Maybe I should ask my Meow employees to do the rest of the investigation. I can give them a raise if they find the murderer. That should be motivation enough. Urgh.

"I find it strange though that he wanted me to give away all the sweets," she suddenly says into the silence. "I would have been able to sell them for a good price or give them to the new owner. Some of the sweet jars were newly refilled, and now they're empty. Those kids have eaten hundreds of darems today."

It must be painful for her to think of that kind of money being given away. She'll be without a job soon, and Mr Kindler didn't leave her anything.

I add it to my list of the strange behaviours of Winston Kindler. It's getting longer the more I find out about him.

"Would you mind if one of my assistants comes here tomorrow to take a look at the files?" I ask her. "That would help you as well, getting some order into this mess."

She looks around the office as if she's only now realising how chaotic everything is.

"It wasn't always this messy," she says quietly. "He used to like everything clean and tidy. Then it all changed a few months ago. As if he no longer cared about the shop's finances. That's when he started talking about selling the shop as well. He'd never mentioned that before. I always thought he'd carry on running this place until he retired."

"A few months ago? Can you remember when exactly?" I ask while making a quick note of what she just said. Finally, something that could qualify as a lead.

She frowns. "It was winter, I remember there being snow. I was thinking how cold it would be if I didn't have this job. Our house is so hard to heat."

Tell me about it. I love having my large house, but it's a pain to keep warm in winter. Wood is expensive to buy in the quantities we need to keep all our fireplaces running.

"January, I think. Yes, it must have been in January."

I smile at her. "Thank you, that really helps. Was there anything else that seemed strange back then?"

Caitlin shakes her head. "No, that's why it was such a shock to hear that he was planning to sell the shop.

There had been no indications before, absolutely nothing. It came out of the blue."

I get up and almost groan as I realise how uncomfortable the chair really was. I'm going to need a stretch after this, or better, a run.

"Let me know if you can think of anything else." I hand her another of my business cards, just in case she lost hers already. "And good luck with finding a new job."

She grimaces. "Thanks. It's not as if this town has a lot of those."

I'm almost out of the door when I turn. "Almost forgot, is there a safe somewhere? I found a key in Mr Kindler's house."

Caitlin shakes her head. "No, we only have the shop, this office, a toilet and a storeroom. There's no space for something as fancy as a safe. He always took our day's earning to the bank in the evening to make sure there was nothing to steal."

"Can I see the storeroom?"

Her expression turns hostile. "No, you can't. Now I think it's better if you leave, you've taken up too much of my time already. I need to clean the shop, and it's late already."

Interesting. I think I know where I'll go tonight. I do love a little breaking and entering.

CHAPTER FIVE

It's raining, but that doesn't stop me from enjoying the run over the rooftops. I could walk on the street like an average person would and then disappear into the shadows once I reach my destination, but that wouldn't be as much fun. I love the way I need to keep my balance, the way the tiles occasionally threaten to slip beneath my feet. It's good training in being silent but fast.

The town looks different from up here. Cleaner, prettier. None of the grime covering the streets. None of the homeless sleeping in dark corners. There are more of those every year. I can't remember ever seeing anyone sleeping rough when I was a child, but now there are too many to count. Sometimes, one of them disappears and is never seen again, but who cares. Nobody but the other homeless, and even those might be glad that they can now take his place. It's a rough world out there. Even though I now have money and a warm home, I still don't feel like I belong. I'm not like the other people living in houses, going to work every day, having a family and a pet. I don't think I'll ever have that, not with the way I was brought up. I never chose to be a killer, but now it's what I am. It's what I'm good at. And I enjoy it. Immensely.

I jump from roof to roof, loving the way it stretches my muscles. I've done too much sitting today. After speaking to Caitlin, I had to spend some time back home in my own office, updating the others and writing some notes. It's a pain in the arse, but I don't want to miss anything that might be glaringly obvious.

Benjamin is going to go to the sweet shop tomorrow to take a look at the finances. He's the brain of Meow - and the best thief. Even if Caitlin is watching, he'll be able to take any folders that may be useful to us. I've told him not to take any money that might be hidden in the lockbox in the bottom drawer, but I know he will do it anyway. It's ingrained in his nature, and I'm really not the right person to judge him for that.

At least it saves me from having to do it. Benjamin is excellent with numbers. If I could trust him not to take half of Meow's company money, he'd do all my finances too. Sadly, I don't trust him. That doesn't mean that he's not my friend.

I come to a halt on the roof opposite the sweet shop and crouch low, scanning the narrow street down below. There's nobody around, not even a cat. I measure the distance. It should work. Climbing down would be so much effort - yeah, jumping it is.

I walk back a few steps and stretch my legs before taking a deep breath. I can do this.

I run and jump, flying through the air, the rain suddenly heavy on my skin as if it's trying to push me down. I just about get a hold of the shop's drain and heave myself up onto the roof. Close call but I made it. As I knew I would. Never doubt your own abilities, that's what I've learned from the very beginning. If you don't think you can kill your mark, you'll make mistakes. If you don't think you can steal something from a watchful person, you'll be caught. Doubting yourself is bad for business. And for your life.

I walk to the edge of the roof where it leads down to a lower building that must have been added as an extension after the shop was built. It's an easy drop although I'm a little worried by the sound the metal roof does when I land on it. I hope it's not too rusty. To avoid any accident, I jump the final stretch, landing in a small backyard. Brick walls loom all around me, but I'm only interested in the iron door that must lead to the storeroom in the extension. The lock is an easy pick that almost disappoints me. I was looking forward to the challenge, but even a baby could do this. An assassin baby, granted, but still. Hopefully, there will be something interesting inside. Caitlin was far too abrupt when I asked to see the storage. There must be something here she doesn't want me to see.

There are no windows, so I don't hesitate flipping the light switch. And stare. I was expecting stacks of boxes, wooden crates, stuff like that, but there's nothing. Nothing except for a thin foam mattress in the centre of the room.

I slowly approach the mattress. It's old and stained

and thinner than it would be comfortable. A smell of stale body odour fills the air around it. I rub my nose and start breathing through my mouth. It seems someone sleeps here regularly, someone who has a disregard for hygiene. It can't be Caitlin. While her clothes were simple, they were also spotless, just like her hair and everything else. So who did sleep here? Winston Kindler? He had his own house, but it didn't look lived in. But come on, who would rather sleep on a dirty mattress in a windowless storeroom than in a pretty little house?

There's a thin grey blanket ruffled up into a ball at the other end of the mattress, but there are no other possessions of the mystery sleeper. No clothes, not even a water bottle. I lift the mattress and check underneath. Bingo. There's a stained envelope, slightly sticky to the touch.

I walk back to the other end of the room where the light is brighter and open the envelope. There's only a small piece of paper in there as well as a black and white photograph. I read the note first.

17 Market Place.
7862
She'll be waiting for you. Come alone.
P.S. 100 children. Don't forget.

I read the message several times. It doesn't make much sense. I better head to Market Place and check out house number 17 to find answers.

The photo's edges are bent and discoloured as if

someone's been holding it a lot. It shows a young woman, maybe my age, with a gentle smile and kind eyes. With her old-fashioned clothes and the fact that the photograph is in black and white, it must be quite old. A few decades at the very least. I run a finger over her bright blonde hair, wondering who she might be. By now she must be an old woman. Her hair will have turned grey, there will be wrinkles on her face. If she's still alive, that is.

I put the photograph and the note back in the envelope and pocket it. I take another quick look around the empty room, but there's nothing here to explore. I'm going to have to return to Caitlin tomorrow and ask her what the hell is going on. Right now, I'm pissed off that she didn't tell me someone was living here. She could have saved me some valuable time. Tomorrow, I'm going to be less friendly to her.

BACK HOME, A CAT IS WAITING FOR ME ON THE FRONT doorstep. I don't think I've seen her before. She's a beautiful dark ginger with fluffy fur that is slightly matted in places.

"You need a good brush," I mutter and bend down to pet her. She purrs and presses against my legs, pushing against my hand when I rub her head. She looks up at me with bright green eyes that convey an intelligence that has me smile. She's no ordinary cat. "Got something for me?" I ask her and she meows.

"Let's get you some food and I might even brush your fur. After you've told me what you know."

She meows her approval and I let her into the house. She heads straight to the kitchen, as if she's been there before. The other cat must have told her what to expect. It seems my spy network is beginning to work. Not that I've had any information from her yet. Maybe she's bluffing. I chuckle to myself. That's exactly what a cat would do.

I put an empty food bowl in front of her, then kneel on the ground until I'm almost at her level.

"I'm going to shift," I warn her. "Don't be scared. I'll be a little bigger than you, but I won't harm you. I just need to be able to talk to you."

She just stares at me. Oh, the arrogance of cats. How dare I imply that she may be scared. Of course, she won't be. She's a cat, a predator, a feline killing machine.

I grin and reach for my panther. She stretches and with a growl, jumps to the surface. I can't suppress a whimper as my body changes. It's a painful but quick shift, its intrinsic magic somehow keeping it without the blood and torn clothes that you'd technically expect when imagining a human turning into a giant black cat. Not that anyone'd really believe that unless they've had contacts with shifters.

When I open my eyes, blinking heavily to adjust to my new, different vision, I'm not surprised to see the ginger cat in exactly the spot she was before I shifted. She looks at me with an almost bored expression. What a poker face.

"What's your name?" I ask, knowing that to any humans that might enter the kitchen, it will sound like a strange mix of growls, chirps and purrs. All cats understand each other, even though there are a variety of dialects.

"Pan," she replies in a melodic but lofty voice. "I was promised food."

I grin. Such confidence. Most humans would be scared of me right now with my sharp claws and my muscular body that screams deadly predator. "You will get it. What do you have for me?"

"The house you went to," she starts, but I interrupt her.

"What house? How do you know that?"

She gives me a blink that equals a human shrug. "Some of us were following you. It's always good to have some intelligence on an employer."

I'm a little stunned by her words. "Wait, you've done this before? You've worked for other people in the past?"

"No, but it's what Ryker said."

"Ryker?"

She sighs. "Pumpkin's father. He was the one who told us that you have jobs going. You gave Pumpkin food this morning, and he vetted you. He said you smelled trustworthy."

"What an honour," I say, sarcasm dripping from my growled words. I've now been labelled trustworthy by a kitten. How lovely.

I lick my paw, remembering how good that feels. I've not spent much time as a jaguar recently. I should really do it more often. Back when my collar was opened, I stayed in my shifted form for two weeks straight. It took that long to familiarise myself with that other 'me' again. I'd been wearing a collar for fifteen years, long enough to almost forget what it was like to explore the world from a non-human perspective.

"After you left, some human men came to the house," Pan says, interrupting my thoughts. Better that way. I don't like being reminded of those dark days. Days that turned into years, into my childhood, my adolescence.

"What did they do?" I ask her before my mind can drift off again.

"Snooped around. Did the same things you did. Looked in the shed, walked through the house. They took less time than you and then left."

"What did they look like? Were they police?"

She sniffs at me. "Police?"

It's as if it hurts her not to know something.

"Were they wearing uniforms?" I try again. "Dark blue uniforms?"

"We don't care about what furs human wear," she replies arrogantly. "But I can ask my sister who was there."

This is becoming complicated. Too many cats, too many names.

"Please do. Can some of you also keep an eye on the sweet shop? There's something suspicious about that place."

"We want daily food deliveries," she demands. "Enough for twenty of us."

I give her a cautionary growl, but she doesn't even

flick her ears. "Twenty? Aren't cats supposed to be solitary creatures?"

"Not since Ryker arrived. He's been bringing us all together, shown us that we can have a better life if we help each other out."

Wow, I need to meet this Ryker. If he's managed to get a bunch of cats to act against their nature, he must be one special beast.

"Food for ten cats, no more, until I know you're worth it." I meet her eyes, showing her that I mean it. There's no bargaining with a jaguar.

It takes her thirty seconds of starting to realise that. Then, finally, she averts her eyes and meows. "Deal. We'll collect it here every morning until we can trust *you* with our location."

Ouch, that hurt.

CHAPTER SIX

"Kat! Come down! You've got visitors!"

I almost fall off my hammock. It feels early, far too fucking early. I got to bed late and usually, the others respect my wish to sleep in. Not today, apparently.

I join Lily in the kitchen, not bothering to change into something more professional than my pyjamas.

"Hole," she says with a grin, pointing at my crotch. Damn, not again. How do I always manage to rip my clothes in indecent places?

I need to stop sitting cross-legged everywhere. It's not good for my clothes bill. If I could sew... well, no, even then I wouldn't have the time nor patience to repair the hole in my pyjama bottoms.

"What's up?" I ask with a yawn while pulling my shirt further down to hide the hole.

"Five cats are waiting outside," she replies with a grin. "I assume that's your doing?"

Ah. Yes. Should have probably told the others what I agreed with the local cat population.

"Meet our latest employees."

She chuckles. "You're actually paying them?"

I shrug and get a mug from the cupboard, taking advantage of the hot water that is still in the kettle.

"I pay them in cat food, they spy for me. I'm doing it as a test run for this case, but if it works, maybe they could become a permanent fixture for Meow. Neither our clients nor our marks would expect the local moggy to be spying for us."

Lily grins wickedly. "Very true. You've told them that they can't expect brushing and massages though, right?"

I don't deign that with a reply and instead pour me a cup of tea.

"Because Ben is out there doing exactly that."

"I thought he didn't like cats," I mutter and take my first sip of tea. Heavenly. It's so hot it burns my gums, but that also means I'm a little more awake now. Pain does that to your brain.

"That's what he says," Lily says with a laugh. "After seeing him surrounded by cats, I no longer believe him. But you know what that also means, right?"

I raise an eyebrow instead of asking what she means.

"He might like you more than he admits, too. After all, you're kind of a cat."

I almost spit out my tea. "You did not just say that."

"That you're an overgrown cat or that he might have a crush on you?"

"Both," I snap.

She laughs again. "Would it be so bad if it was true? He's handsome in a boyish sort of way."

I snort. "Exactly. He's far too young for me. He still needs to grow his adult whiskers."

"We've resorted to cat metaphors now, have we?" she mocks, grinning widely. "That's usually a sign that you're lying."

I take another sip of tea, loving the way the hot liquid runs down into my stomach. It makes me feel alive.

"He's too young," I repeat. "Besides, I don't have time for stuff like that. I have a murder to solve and then, once this case is finally done, a murder to cause. Or two. I already miss that line of work. This detective thing really isn't for me."

She looks at me with a hint of sympathy. "Need any help?"

"Actually, yes. The brother of the guy who died. Can you get close to him? Find out if there's anything he might not have told me? There are so many question marks surrounding the murder that I'm having trouble trusting anything I've been told."

"Sure thing. Is he hot?"

I sigh. "Are you sure you're not an incubus?"

Lily laughs. "Those don't exist. I'm just a sexually liberated woman who knows what to do with her womanly wiles."

This time, I really do snort into my mug. "Womanly wiles? Are you for real?"

"Real as it gets. And what's most important, my boobs are real too. Men like that. Anyway, give me the guy's address, and I'll do some investigating." She gives me a saucy wink. "Now go and talk to the cats. Or Ben. Or both."

She shoos me out of the kitchen - *my* kitchen - and I find myself face to face with our thief. He's covered in cat hair and has something of a crazy grin on his face.

"There are cats outside," he tells me as if that isn't obvious by now.

"I know. Did you feed them yet?"

He blushes. "I did. Wasn't I supposed to?"

I laugh. "No, that was exactly what you were supposed to do. Tell you what, from now on, you're responsible for feeding the cats every morning. It's going to be ten of them, so you better order some more cat food. Clear?"

He groans but then nods. "Aye aye. Now I need a shower though. I can't do my job if I smell of cat."

I laugh as he walks away, muttering to himself.

I found him pretty early on in my business venture. He tried to steal my bag and failed, obviously. He was also on the run from the Pack, just like I was. Except that he was alone on the streets while I had a house, money and an anonymous benefactor. I made him prove that he was good at picking pockets, then I took him on as an employee. It's worked out well for both of us, but what I told Lily was right. He's too young for me. Two years younger than me at the very least and I'm not into that. I prefer men over boys. Men who know where to stick it and don't have to fumble around helplessly.

Meow!

One of the cats sticks his head through the open door, glaring at me. Did I do something wrong?

"Good morning," I tell him and follow him outside. There are eight other cats spread out across the stone steps leading up to the door, all of them busy either eating or licking their fur. My skin begins to itch at that sight. I love doing that myself when I'm shifted. Lying in the sun, grooming myself, snoozing the day away... cats have the perfect life. Sadly, I'm only partly like them. I rarely have the time to relax. There is always work to do. Even now, I can't stay to watch them play.

"Do I need to shift?" I ask the male cat who's still staring at me. "Is there something I need to know?"

He meows and I hear the negation in his voice. Good, saves me from using up energy on shifting.

"Then eat something and don't bother me," I tell him, realising that I never got to finish my tea. I've not had breakfast yet, either. Mornings are cruel.

The cat gives me a glare and then struts away with a swagger, not sparing me a second glance. I wonder if this is Ryker.

Reassured that the cats have all they need and demand, I change clothes and make myself a sandwich, intending to eat it on the way. Before I leave, I make sure that both Lily and Benjamin know what they're doing today, then I head off towards the market.

OF COURSE, I HAD TO PICK MARKET DAY. THE ENTIRE square is full of stalls and people, battering against my senses. I tone down my panther abilities as much as possible. The stink of the town would be unbearable otherwise. I never buy from the market, not when I can smell the first signs of decay on the meat, the scent of mould on vegetables. Nothing here is good quality, and yet people buy it because it makes them feel better than going to the shops. The market is just a front for some of the town's shadier dealings, but of course, most people don't know that. They think they're supporting their local businesses, while in fact, they're giving money to drug dealers and smugglers. They don't know that sometimes, their fruit smell like dead bodies and that the apple they eat may have been in contact with a victim of violence. It's a strange place, this market.

Number 17 is a tall, imposing building at the edge of the market square; far enough not to get the smells and the noise but close enough to see what may be going on. There are multiple names on the sign outside, none of which ring any bells. I write them all down just in case, maybe one of them will make sense later. I try the door and surprisingly, it's open. Taking a quick look around to see if anyone's watching me, I step inside.

The stairwell is pleasantly cool. The staircase winds around a single marble column that runs all the way up to the top floor. It reeks of money.

All I have to go on is a string of numbers. 7862. Maybe there's a flat 7? I'm rather hoping of finding a door with a keypad, however. That would be much more fun.

Inspecting each and every door, I slowly work my way up. On the third floor, I find a broom cupboard squeezed in between flats 5 and 6. Sadly, there's nothing inside except for a rather large spider who's turned the little room into a work of art.

"Well done," I whisper and close the door behind me, leaving her to it.

One floor up, I can't help but smile in excitement. There's not just a flat 7, but there's also a keypad. Two in one. Finally, something good happens.

I press my ear against the wooden door, listening for any sounds on the other side. Nothing. I close my eyes and extend my senses as far as I can, searching for any signs of life. There is someone in flat 8 next door, but not in the one I'm about to enter.

I open my eyes again and key in the number. 7862. A little green light blinks twice, and the lock opens with a click. I'm in.

Before I enter, I scan the hallway in front of me. There could be traps, who knows. By now, with so many strange clues and contradictions, in this case, I'm prepared for anything and everything.

Slowly, I make my way forward, keeping all my senses on high alert. I'm not in the mood for nasty surprises. The first room on the left is a kitchen. I give it a quick search. It's empty, no pots and pans, not even cutlery. The fridge isn't even on. What's strange though is that there is no dust. The place looks like nobody is using it, but it must have been cleaned recently. Maybe someone is going to sell it?

Connected by an open doorframe is a small dining room. There are burn stains on the large dinner table, but the cabinets lying the walls are empty. I check the undersides of the chairs and table, behind the shelves, everywhere, but I don't find anything. No secret notes, no bundles of cash, no locked doors. My mind is telling me to relax, but I don't. Something about this place is giving me the creeps.

The next room is completely empty. No furniture, just some discolouration of the walls where furniture must have stood at some point. There are traces of mould in one corner. There's a huge red rug in the centre of the room, but nothing underneath. Pity, I was kind of hoping for a trap door. Did I mention that I love trap doors? If my house didn't already have one, I would have installed one after moving in.

The bathroom is just as uninteresting. The toilet looks disgusting and completely the opposite of the clean kitchen. Stains of body fluids are everywhere. There's a stench in the air that makes me want to puke. I hold my breath as I lift the lid with disgust scrunching my features. And almost puke when I see the glass jar sitting at the bottom of the toilet. Yuck. I wish I'd brought gloves. Well, I'm wearing leather gloves, but I'm not getting those dirty. They're my favourite pair.

Luckily, I find some rubber gloves in the kitchen together with a bucket. Back in the bathroom, I switch on the fan, hoping that it will make the smell a little less intense. Ignoring the urge to throw up, I plunge my hand into the brown water and pull out the glass, immediately putting it in the sink to clean it of all the... things sticking to it. Whoever thought it would be a good idea to hide something in the toilet?

I keep the tap switched on even after the jar looks

clean. I don't want some nameless people's shit on my hands.

Now that all the dirt has washed away, I can finally look inside. There's a rolled up paper, and inside of it, I can just about make out some bank notes. I gently shake the glass and it makes a clunky sound. There's something metal inside.

Satisfied that it won't get any cleaner, I switch off the tap and open the lid of the glass jar, careful not to let any water drip on the paper. I decide it's time to leave the bathroom and return to the kitchen, grateful for its cleanliness. I've never been a clean freak, but there are certain minimum standards that I value. Like a toilet that isn't full of faeces and dried piss.

After drying the glass with a tea towel I find at the bottom of one drawer, I get to work, carefully pouring the contents on the kitchen counter. Besides the paper and a large bunch of money, a key and two large coins fall out.

I'm kind of expecting a love letter, an order to assassinate someone, or some other juicy content, but the letter is as boring as this entire case. It's an invoice. A bloody invoice. And it's all sweets. The list would make my mouth water if I hadn't just had my hand inside a toilet. Mint humbugs, acid drops, liquorice curls, sherbet lemons... This is any child's dream. I bet those are the same sweets Mr Kindler sold. It's definitely a link to the case, but I can't get my head around the fact that someone thought this invoice important enough to hide it. For me, it looks normal. The quantities aren't exciting, nor are the cost prices. I shrug and decide to let

Benjamin take a look at it. Maybe he can spot something I don't.

I won't show him the money though, or it would be gone immediately. It's at least a thousand darems. To be honest, this case is becoming slightly profitable on so many levels.

The key is similar to the one I found in Winston's remote control. I rummage in my bag until I find that one and compare the two. No, they're not similar, they're identical, down to the smallest tooth.

How very strange. Finally, I take a look at the two coins. They're the same. A bronze coin with a square in the centre that's cut through in the middle with a sharp vertical dash. No idea what that's supposed to mean. They don't look like they could be currency from abroad; there are no numbers on them to indicate their value. Besides, they almost look handmade judging from the slight differences in weight.

I put everything in my bag and go through the flat one last time. Maybe I've missed something. I really hope so because otherwise, I'm back to square one.

Four rooms. One of them empty, one of them clean, one of them dirty and the fourth somewhere in between. Something is missing. No bedroom. And now that I think about it, the layout of the flat doesn't make sense. There are more rooms on the left of the hallway than on the right. There must be a large empty space there that isn't being used. Please let it be a hidden room, please. That would make my day.

CHAPTER SEVEN

I hold my breath and go back into the bathroom, the only room to the right. There are only a toilet and a sink, no shower or bathtub. Again, that feels strange. How are people living in this flat supposed to wash? There is however a full-length mirror on the right wall. I inspect it from all sides, then push the edges. When I press my fingers on the wooden surrounding on the left, there's a visible click. Like a lock springing open. I grip the wood with my fingernails and pull. Tada! There's a door behind it. Success. Finally.

Leaving the smelly bathroom behind, I step into a dark room. I switch on my torch and can't find a light switch, but there's a window with the curtains drawn. I pull them open, letting light in. Wow. I did not expect this.

Two metal tables are in the centre, strange appliances and tools strewn on top of them. My training kicks in and before I go and explore, I circle the room, looking for alarms, traps or anything else that could inconvenience me. Besides a narrow crate full of knives beneath a shelf – an assassin's wet dream – there are no dangerous things in the room.

I grin and head towards my prize, the tables in the centre of the room. There is a strange white powder everywhere. Sugar? Something more sinister?

I take a tiny glass jar from my bag and brush some powder in there. I'm going to test it later on at home. I'm good with poisons, and I bet I'm going to find out what this is.

I recognise some of the tools on the tables from my own kitchen, but others I don't know. It looks a bit like a mixture of a bakery and a pharmacy. Vials with liquids of various colours, metal shapes that remind me of the ones you can use to make your own chocolates, bowls with whisks and scrapers and in the middle of it all, a cardboard box full of plastic bags. Which are filled with white powder. The same one that's scattered all over the table, I bet. I pocket one of them, careful to wrap it in a second bag, just in case. If this is some kind of poison, I don't want it contaminating everything in my bag.

There are no gloves or protective gear anywhere in the room, which makes me think that it's not a poison that acts through the skin. Maybe ingestion? Or mix it with water and inject it? I can't wait to get back home to my lab and experiment.

I spend the next two hours meticulously searching the room. I pocket some invoices and order forms for various ingredients – none of them suspicious but you never know – and take a few books from a shelf. Two of them are romance novels, and I bet the people who worked here weren't into that kind of book. There must be something interesting in them, but I don't want to linger here too long. The disadvantage with taking them is that whoever owns this place will know that I was here, but that's a risk I'm willing to take.

I'm almost ready to go when I open the bottom doors of a pretty wooden cabinet. Inside is a fridge. What the hell… Why hide it in a cupboard? There's another, larger fridge on the other end of the room, but that one was empty. This one, however, isn't.

Some people would scream. Others would stagger back in shock. Me? I take the bloody hand and inspect it curiously. It's a woman's left hand, intact besides the fact that it's no longer attached to its body. The nails are perfectly manicured, and I admire the red varnish for a moment. Not that I'd ever wear that sort of thing, but I can appreciate it on others.

None of the nails are chipped or broken, and there's nothing beneath them. She didn't fight. Either because she was surprised, unconscious, dead or because her hands were bound.

She'll be waiting for you. The note is now making more sense. Was she still alive when Winston Kindler – or whoever the message was intended for – was supposed to come to this place? Or was she already dead?

I no longer consider this case boring. I have a mutilated hand. It makes me so happy.

"I found a hand!" I cheerily tell Lily as soon as I

enter the kitchen. "We really need to get the cooling room fixed."

"*You* need to get it fixed," she scoffs but then points at my backpack. "Show me."

I take it out and Lily takes it, her face lighting up like I just gave her a birthday present. I make a mental note. It's her birthday in two months, and if she likes a hand this much, I might get her one. By then, I'll be back to killing rather than solving murders, and a dead body won't miss his hand. I just need to find out if she prefers male or female hands.

"Look what the cat's dragged in," she mutters under her breath as she examines the hand, turning it around, inspecting it from all angles. "Where did you get it?"

"Found it in a fridge."

She laughs. "See, other people keep body parts in their fridges too! I'll tell you that next time you admonish me for it."

"They don't have a morgue," I snap with a grin. "I also found some money, so I'm going to commission the repairs tonight."

"Want me to take a look at the hand in the meantime? It looks like it was cut off when the woman was already dead, but I can do some tests to confirm that."

I really want to refuse her offer – how often do I get to play with a body part not attached to a person – but I know I need to do other things first.

I sigh. "Go ahead and take this powder with you, it needs analysing. I've also got some random romance novels for you that might have some hidden messages inside. Unless one of our killers likes to read about a widower having a relationship with two sisters. I'll join you downstairs in a moment, I need to talk to the cats first and organise the repairs. Is Benjamin back yet?"

She nods. "He's in his room. Beth is here as well, she's in the living room eating copious amounts of crisps."

I've not seen Beth in days. She does that. Disappears without explanation, then comes back with three or more marks ticked off the list. Then she takes a week off, relaxing and eating junk food. It's a strange way of working, but as long as she does her job, I don't care.

"I'll check in on her. Maybe she has some time to help out with this case."

Lily snickers. "Beth? Help out? You know she's not going to move off that sofa for the next twenty-four hours at the very least."

"I'm sure I can find a way to incentivise her," I scoff. "And if it means taking her crisps away."

My friend laughs. "Good luck with that. How do you want to be buried? Cremation?"

I flip her off and leave the room, heading to the office first. One phone call later, I've arranged for workmen to come and fix the cooling room. They're from a company I've used before; people who know when to speak and when to stay silent. Coupled with a large tip, they won't mention this house having an extensive morgue to anyone. And if they do… well, I do love a vengeful assassination.

Just like Lily said, Benjamin is in his room. He's sitting cross-legged on the floor, papers strewn all around him. I stay by the door, not wanting to distract him too much.

"Find anything?" I ask and he looks up with a small smile.

"I think so. I've been going through Kindler's bank statements and it's quite fascinating. His only source of income should be the earnings he makes with the shop, right?"

"As far as I know, yes. I've not found anything of a second job, and besides, he wouldn't have had the time for that."

Benjamin nods. "That's what I thought, but he gets a payment into his account every week. Not massive amounts, but they add up to quite a nice sum. Another strange thing is that he never pays his bills in full."

"Explain," I demand.

He takes one of the sheets of papers and hands it to me. "That's an invoice for chocolate bars. 723 darems. But he never paid that much for it." He points at another letter. "He only paid 410 darems. And that's just one example. As far as I can see, he never paid in full for sweets. He did, however, pay his electricity and gas bills in full. Same with insurance."

"Maybe he had a special deal with his supplier?" I suggest.

Benjamin shakes his head. "That would have been on the invoices. It would make sense for tax reasons. And to make it easier. If the supplier doesn't want the full amount, then why not just put it on the invoice that way? No, I think he was getting a discount for something he did. Something that nobody wanted to keep a record of. Together with those weekly payments… I think he was corrupt. He accepted money for something he did, something illegal."

"But what would a sweet shop owner do that would have to be kept secret?" I ask, more to myself than to him. "His only customers were children or maybe parents. Not exactly the right customer base."

He shrugs. "Drugs, maybe? But it's your job to figure that out. I'm just giving you the facts."

I sigh. "Okay, write down the details of his suppliers, and I'll pay them a visit tomorrow."

He rummages around and pulls an envelope from his paper mess. "Here's one already. I'll give you the others later on, there are a few more things I want to check."

I take the envelope and stare at the address. 17 Market Place.

You must be kidding me.

CHAPTER EIGHT

Two cats are lounging in our garden. Well, the garden is not much more than a place to keep our bins and a small stretch of grass, but the cats seem to enjoy the warm stones. Hell, I would do the same if I had the time. I've done that before, shifted and then relaxed in the sun. Nobody from the surrounding houses can look into the backyard so I wouldn't have to explain why a big black panther is hanging out in our garden.

One of the cats is the little kitten, Pumpkin. He meows and jumps off one of the bins, rubbing against my legs.

"Hello, little one," I mutter and scratch him behind his ears. He immediately starts purring.

The other cat is one I haven't seen before. It's a female, black as the night, with a few white spots on her forehead that remind me of stars. She's stunning with her silky fur and her bright yellow eyes.

"And who are you?" I ask, even though I won't

understand her answer anyway without being shifted. She just continues to stare at me. "Do I need to shift?"

All I get from her is indifference. I turn to Pumpkin who's still enjoying a head rub.

"I've got a new job for you and the others. Can you take a look around the market place, see if you find anything. A dead woman, maybe. Or something else that's suspicious. Do you understand?"

He rubs against my leg and sends his assent. Good. Now I have my own personal sniffer cats. If anyone can find a hidden corpse, they can. Even if I was to shift to use my superior panther nose, I'd never get into tight spaces like they can, and besides, there's a bounty on uncollared shifters. If I want to keep my independence, I need to stay low and pretend to be human. Luckily, there aren't many cat shifters, so people have grown better at spotting canine shifters. If I was a wolf or dog... well, let's just say I wouldn't be living in this town.

I give Pumpkin one last cuddle and go back inside to search out Beth. Not that there's any searching involved. She's sprawled out on the sofa, two empty crisp packets on her chest.

"Morning," she mutters with a yawn when I wave at her.

"Morning?" I scoff. "It's late afternoon. I've been out all day."

She shrugs and lazily closes her eyes again. "It feels like morning. Can you close the door behind you?"

I sigh. "Beth, we need to have a chat."

"Not in the mood," she groans. "I need some peace

and quiet. I killed two people last night, I've deserved a break."

I'm almost jealous at that. Instead of sneaking through abandoned flats and looking at sweet shops, she actually got to have some fun. *Remember the money, Kat. Remember the money.*

The doorbell rings and Beth snickers. "Guess I'll get my break after all."

I frown at her. "We'll have a Meow meeting in two hours in here. Don't leave, we need all of us there."

She shrugs and opens a third crisp bag, while I sigh and leave the room.

Three workmen are waiting in front of the house, all of them carrying tool boxes and other things that are probably meant to look professional. I lead them down into the basement, glad that Lily seems to have closed all the doors to rooms that may contain the more incriminating parts of our job. Like body parts, skeletons and the poison lab. To be honest, most of the skeletons were already there when we moved in. We've only added a few. Usually, we leave our bodies where we killed them. No need in dragging them all the way here just to store them in the basement.

"Need anything?" I ask them when I've shown them the cooling room.

One of them - probably the boss - looks around and shakes his head. "We'll call if we do."

I nod and leave them alone, although I've got my cat senses on high alert. If they move to another room or sneak around, I'll know.

I tell Lily and Benjamin about our Meow meeting,

then head to my office, already dreading the paperwork that's waiting there for me. When did life become so complicated?

"Feet off the table," Lily snaps, and to my surprise, Beth lifts her legs and sits down properly, although she does it with a self-pitying groan. We've not been in one room all together for ages. While I always know what everyone's up to - I hand out the tasks, after all - we rarely meet up to discuss one particular case. If someone needs help, they come to me or ask one of the others who has a specific expertise. Benjamin for theft, Lily for seduction and deceit, Beth for poisons and antidotes. We're a great team except that we don't really work as a team. I make a mental note to change that. Maybe I should do a team building exercise or something... kill a target together. Who can kill the fastest? Find the prettiest dead body?

"Why are we here?" Beth asks with a yawn. "I will have you know that my brain is still in snooze mode. If you have something important to say, write it down and I'll review it when I'm more awake."

I glare at her. "You're going to listen and take part in this meeting like everyone else," I tell her with as much authority as I can muster. "Or you can see how you cope with half your pay this month."

She stares back defiantly, but I'm already turning away, looking at the other two. They're much easier to handle.

"I've called in this meeting to discuss the Kindler case," I begin. "Beth, you won't know about this yet so here's a quick recap. Winston Kindler is-"

"Was," Lily corrects.

"-was a sweet shop owner who was murdered a couple of days ago. We've not seen the body, and it's unlikely that we will as the police have it under lock and key. It seems to have been bloody though."

"I could try and sneak in," Benjamin suggests. "It's worth a try."

I nod. "If you want, but don't complain if you get caught. They improved their security measures since the last time you broke in."

He shrugs with a smug grin. "I bet they're not good enough to keep me out. They'd have to be reaaally good, and I highly doubt that. The police don't have enough money."

He's right about that.

"Okay, do it and let me know what you find." I take out the file Mr Kindler's brother gave me and go over the information we already have. "He was killed just outside the sweet shop in the early morning before it opened. No witnesses, at least none who have come forward. When I went to the shop, there were no traces left, no scents either. The police believe it was a mugging and have stopped investigating, but still have the body. That's why we've been given this case by the victim's brother. He's not satisfied with the police's work and is willing to pay us a lot of money to find the killer."

"How much?" Beth asks, suddenly very awake.

I grin. "Enough to give us all a holiday, fix up the house and then some."

A sly smile spreads on her face. "Why didn't you say so? I'm in."

"Didn't you say we're allowed to exterminate the killer?" Lily asks and I nod.

"Yes, but first we need to find him. It's all a bit complicated. Let's start with the shop. The only employee is a young girl called Caitlin. Mr Kindler made her promise to give away all the sweets for free in the case of his death. She did that yesterday, and I think every single child in this town went there to get some free tooth decay."

"Could have brought me some," Beth mutters.

I ignore her. "Benjamin has found some interesting things in the shop's office though, right?"

He nods. "Basically, Winston Kindler got some anonymous payments and never paid his invoices in full. It seems people were giving him money, but there's no record of why they did that. What they got in return."

"I visited his house," I continue, "and there were even more riddles there. A key hidden in a remote control and a number scrawled on a lawnmower cord. Then in the storcroom behind the shop, I found a mattress. Someone's been sleeping there. I'm going to find Caitlin and ask her about that. There was also a note that led me to a flat by the market square."

I take out the items I recovered from the toilet, minus the money. That's already in my safe. If I showed it to these three, it would be gone immediately.

"I found these in the toilet."

Lily laughs. "Seriously? They look rather clean."

"In a glass jar," I clarify.

Benjamin immediately snaps the invoice while Beth takes one of the coins, twirling it between her fingers. "I've seen these before," she mutters. "But I can't remember where."

"Try to," I say, not unkindly.

Lily is looking at the key. "Do you have the one you found in the victim's house?" she asks and I hand it to her.

"They may look different but they're for the same lock," she says slowly. "Any idea what door these might open?"

I shake my head. "I didn't find a locked door in his house or the flat. Not in the shop, either. It must be somewhere we haven't been yet."

"I remember!" Beth suddenly shouts, making all of us look at her. "But you're not going to like the answer."

I sigh. "Tell us."

"The Fangs."

Lily sucks in a deep breath. "Please tell me that's a joke," she whispers, her eyes wide.

Beth shrugs. "I can if you want me to lie."

"What are the Fangs?" Benjamin asks. I'm glad he does. I've heard of them, but I don't know enough.

"In this town, we have the Pack," Beth begins to explain. "Some may call them a crime organisation, the mafia, but we all know that they're funded by the town council. They keep control of any shifters that are found."

I realise that I'm rubbing my throat and immediately

put my hands in my lap, shocked by my lack of awareness. I don't move my body without wanting to. My body is a weapon, trained since childhood to be as dangerous as it can be. I ball my hands into fists. I don't want to think of the Pack, but it seems they're somehow involved in all this.

Lily gives me a small smile, knowing exactly what I'm thinking. She knows my history, and while I've never told the other two, I'm sure they do too. They know I'm a shifter, and the chances of there being a shifter who hasn't been part of the Pack are slim, to say the least.

"The Pack is like the baby brother of the Fangs," Beth continues. "They're active all over the country, not just this town. Nobody ever sees them, but they monitor everything. They have influence on the highest and the lowest level. If a Fang wants you dead, you're dead. They'll never dirty their own hands, they'll simply tell the regional groups to do it. Like the Pack, in our case."

"If they're that powerful, why have I never heard of them?" Benjamin asks.

"Because you've always worked independently," Lily replies. "You've not been a part of one of the gangs. They wouldn't be interested in a lone thief. No, they prefer to exert their influence on an entire group like the Pack. It's more efficient."

"Sometimes, we knew that the tasks we were given hadn't come from our Pack leaders," I say quietly, pushing through the memories that I try so hard to forget. "A lot of them weren't about killing, they were about intimidation. About making an example of someone. The Pack rarely told us to be brutal, they wanted clean efficiency. The Fangs are different."

Beth nods. "And they use these coins as tokens to show that they're either a Fang themselves or in their direct employ. I once found a coin like this on a mark. When I showed it to my employer, he looked at it as if it was a poisonous snake and then tried to kill me." She shrugs. "He obviously didn't succeed, but he did use his last words to warn me. To get rid of the coin and never talk about it again."

A cold shiver runs over my back. "The question is, what does a sweet shop owner have to do with the Fangs? Or even the Pack? If we ignore the hidden keys and the fact that his house looked unlived in, he seems completely normal and boring."

"Exactly the point," Lily says. "It's all a facade. For all we know, he could have been a Fang. Using the sweet shop to launder money, using children as his messengers. If you use cats, why shouldn't he use children?"

I shake my head. "I can't imagine Winston Kindler being a Fang. Not from what I've heard about him so far."

Lily shrugs. "Let's keep an open mind. Anything else you've found?"

"I think that's everything. Besides the hand that's now in our newly repaired cooling room."

I kind of expect applause, but nobody reacts. "Newly repaired," I repeat. "Great news!"

"Uh uh," Beth mutters. "I never use that room anyway. I'd be more excited if you'd bought me some new toys for the lab."

"Don't forget the powder," Lily reminds me. "I've checked it for the standard poisons, but no matches so far."

Beth perks up. "Powder?"

I nod. "In the market place flat, they seem to have been making some kind of white powder. Could be a poison, a drug, even some kind of medicine, who knows. I gave Lily a sample."

Beth frowns in annoyance. "Why not me?"

"Because I thought you'd be busy relaxing on the sofa for the next twenty-four hours at the very least," I say with a dramatic sigh. "Was I wrong?"

Beth grins. "Let's see who of us will identify it sooner. Lily may have had a head start, but I'm better."

The two women glare at each other, but both are smiling. I don't mind a bit of friendly competition, it probably gets the job done quicker.

"Good, you two explore the powder, and Benjamin can take a look at the corpse. Me, I'm going to examine the hand. Tomorrow, I'll seek out Caitlin and talk to the cats, maybe some of them have found something interesting."

"Wow, we're so organised," Benjamin says with a grin. "That's never happened before."

I shrug. "Maybe that's what Meow was always supposed to be. Private investigators rather than assassins."

Beth yawns. "No, don't say that. I'd die of boredom without the killing."

CHAPTER NINE

Lily was right. The hand was cut off when the victim was already dead. That means we're not looking after a handless woman but a handless body. Hopefully, the cats will find the rest of her. Unless she's been cut into several pieces. I hope not. That would take forever.

I test the few traces of blood still within the hand for poison. Nothing. That means she was probably killed by other means - or died of natural causes. Judging from the perfect condition of her skin and bones though, she seems to have been in good health. She must have been in her thirties, maybe early forties; not exactly an age where people tend to drop like flies.

I do some more tests, then put the hand in the cooling room which has been left slightly dirty but very nice and cold by the workers. Maybe I can persuade one of the others to wipe the floor in here. Perks of being their employer, right?

I lock up behind me and check on Lily and Beth,

who're both in the lab, playing with the white powder I gave them.

"Identified it yet?" I ask in passing.

"Nope," Beth grinds out while holding a pipette between her teeth. Not sure that's safe but she must know what she's doing.

"Go have fun with the cats," Lily says with a grin, knowing exactly what I'm itching to do. "I'll write you a note if we find something."

"Meow," Beth snickers and I'm tempted to throw something at her.

Instead, I leave them alone and check the backyard. No cats there this time. None on the steps in front of the house either. I whistle a couple of times, but they're either hiding or simply not here. I smile. It's time for a game of hide and seek.

I PROWL THE ROOFS, FOLLOWING THE SCENT OF ONE OF the cats. It's a female one, but I've not been introduced to her yet. I thought it would be more fun to search for her rather than one I've already met. If I want to work with these cats on a regular basis, I'll have to get to know them. I snicker, a growl escaping my furry chest. I now have not only three human employees (although I still think Lily has a bit of incubus blood in her), but also an army of cats. Let's see who will be the bigger help in finding Winston Kindler's killer. I've got my money on the cats, just saying. I may be prejudiced though.

The wind is cool against my black fur and I breathe

in deep, enjoying the fresh air. Everything is so much sharper, so much more alive. It's hard to believe that humans will never know how much of the world they're missing. All these sounds, the smells, the way a roof feels beneath paws. The feeling of falling from height only for the body to know exactly how to right itself, then land on all four paws. My cat body is a true miracle, and I can't help but appreciate it, despite all the trouble I've had because I was born a shifter. It's worth it for moments like these. Complete freedom, nothing to stop me from doing what I want.

I almost forget that I've got a task to do tonight. Still, I better see the cats now and then spend some more time running around. If there's time, I might leave the town and run in the forest on the other side of the river. It's much nicer to have forest floor beneath my paws rather than dirty roofs and pavements.

The scent slowly becomes stronger the further I get. The trail is leading away from the centre of town, into the poorer outskirts. I don't come here very often. The people I'm paid to dispose of usually live in the more affluent parts. There's a reason they need to be killed: money, inheritances, revenge. Besides, people in this area wouldn't be able to afford my services.

I hear the cats before I can smell or see them. Two of them, both female. Moaning. Not in pain. In love. Seriously? Did I stumble across a cat date? Just my luck. I jump from one low roof to another and then use some bins as a stepping stone to get down to the ground. I'm in a paved backyard full of rubbish bags and rat droppings. There are more romantic places for a date, that much is for sure.

I clear my throat - which sounds like thunder breaking over arid land - and wait for them to emerge from the shadows. A growl answers me, and a second later, I'm faced by two cats. The one on the left is the one whose scent I've been following. She's a chubby tabby; a cat nobody would look twice at in the street. Not particularly beautiful but with fierce eyes that challenge me to explain why I'm interrupting her. The other cat is more elegant with silky black fur and a golden stripe on her forehead as if painted on with a brush.

"What do you want?" the black cat snaps, her voice surprisingly deep. "Can't you see we're busy?"

I smile at her, exposing my very large, very sharp teeth.

"That's Kat," the tabby says before I can reply. "She's the one I told you about. I was going to take you there for breakfast tomorrow morning, Shara, so don't be rude."

"Breakfast." Shara licks her mouth. "Are you taking me on another date?"

For a moment, I'm imagining the two lounging on a picnic blanket in my garden, candles and rosebuds all around them. Maybe I should organise that, just for fun.

"Perhaps." The tabby cat turns to me. "How can we help?"

"What's your name?" I ask, remembering to keep my voice low. I don't want any of the humans to think that they have a panther in their backyard. It would be true, obviously, but... well, let's not.

"Milena, but you may call me Mila," she says haughtily.

I decide to skip the pleasantries and go straight to business. Cats aren't into small talk. They prefer to scratch before they tell you why.

"Have you found anything? Any dead bodies? Any suspicious humans around the market place?"

To my surprise, it's Shara who replies. "Yes, Storm mentioned she'd found a few dead humans." She starts licking her paws to make it clear how boring she's finding it all.

"Why didn't anyone tell me?" I ask, trying to keep the annoyance out of my voice. Not easy when your body loves to growl.

"Ryker was going to come to your house tomorrow," Mila says. "It's not like the bodies are getting any deader."

She's got a point, but they don't understand that decomposition makes it a lot harder to examine a corpse. If I want to have a good chance of determining how and when they died, it's vital that I see them now. "Bodies? How many?"

The cats look at each other. "A pawful? But Storm is polydactyl so it could be up to six."

Six bodies! So much fun to be had in the morgue. The others are going to be ecstatic. Now I'm really glad that I got the cooling room fixed. We're going to need it.

"Where do I find Storm?" I ask, almost bouncing with excitement.

"In our home." Mila sighs. "Which you're not allowed to see. We'll tell her to meet you at the market square."

"Good. Go and tell her now, please."

"Will there be salmon for breakfast?" Shara asks in return.

I can only shake my head. Cats.

I DON'T HAVE TO WAIT LONG FOR STORM TO FIND ME. She's absolutely stunning. Silky black fur hides her in the shadows, but her striking azure eyes give her away, reflecting the moonlight. I take a quick peek at the sky. Almost full moon, maybe two more days. That's the day I don't shift and don't go outside. It's the only night of the month that some of the most powerful Pack members take off their collars and run free. I never had that privilege, but I've heard of what happens from others in the Pack. Sex, drugs and death. Minus the drugs, I think. Being without a collar is drug enough, especially if you're not used to it.

I rub my neck. It's been half a year now, and it feels both longer and shorter at the same time. I don't miss the Pack; it never felt anything else than a prison to me. Others had friends there, but not me. I was different from the start: not a wolf or a dog, but a cat. I smelled different. People were aggressive towards me without even knowing why themselves. It's the scents. Cats and dogs will always be at odds.

Without a meow, Storm beckons me to follow her.

I'm back to human; here in this busy part of town, it's much harder to evade curious eyes. If I need to talk to Storm, I'll search out a quiet corner or backyard and shift there.

She leads me away from the square and into a dark alleyway. During the day, this place is full of people heading to the market, but right now, we're the only ones walking through the darkness. A single street lamp throws a small circle of light onto the cobblestones, but both Storm and I have no problem seeing at night.

She stops in front of an old house. It's nothing special, maybe a bit shabbier than its neighbours, but it wouldn't stand out if I walked past it in daylight. On the left side of the house, steps lead down into what I assume is the basement, or perhaps a flat beneath the main house. Storm stops on the top step and nods towards the metal door at the bottom. Is this where the corpses are hidden? It would certainly be a good location.

The door is locked. I look back at Storm, but she's just sitting there, still as a statue, not giving me any indication of how the cats would have got in to find the bodies. I concentrate on my panther senses and sniff the air. There's a tiny trace of something sweet. Decay. Seems I'm in the right place.

I take out my lock picks and get to work. For a door to a basement, it's a surprisingly complicated lock. It takes me almost a minute to pick, which really says a lot. I'm good with locks. Excellent, actually.

. . .

As soon as I open the door, a lamp inside switches on automatically. I shield my eyes from the bright light, but luckily, I already know that there's nobody in the room. I would have smelled them when I did my panther sniff. I grin at my choice of words. That should become an expression. Kat's panther sniff.

Luckily, I work alone. There's nobody here to tell me off for thinking inappropriate thoughts while staring at four corpses. Two female, two male. All of them lie on metal tables as if they're waiting to be cut open. Or butchered. Depends on the criminal, I guess.

There's not much in the room beside the four large tables. A couple of metal shelves line the wall furthest from the door, and there's a desk to my right. Without a chair. Probably used to put things on rather than to write. A few papers and notes are scattered all across it, but I decide to do the fun part first: looking at the bodies.

The one closest to me is a woman with a missing hand. Bingo. She's intact otherwise, although there are thick purple bruises around her neck. Strangled. I walk closer and run a finger over her cold skin. The first signs of decomposition have already appeared, but she can't have been dead for more than two days or so. It's cold in this basement, which makes calculating it more difficult than if she'd stayed outside. Although maybe she died down here. I'm not an expert in analysing corpses. I know the basics, but usually, I don't really care what happens to the bodies after I relieve them of life.

Her hand has been cleanly sawed off. I almost admire the way the edges of her skin are smooth and that the bones aren't splintered. Whoever did this used some proper tools and didn't do it in a hurry. This was a professional at work. Maybe I'll get to meet them, compare notes. Excitement bubbles up in me until I remember that I'm here to find the killer, not fraternise with them.

There is nothing on the naked woman's body that could give me any clue to who killed her. I mean, I didn't really expect that - assassins rarely leave their name tattooed on the victim's skin - but it's still disappointing. Who is she? How is she connected to Mr Kindler? And why her hand? It must have been intended as a message for the sweet shop owner, but did he ever receive it? Did he get to the flat in the market square to see the hand before he was killed? So many questions and I'm still no closer to any answers.

With a sigh, I turn away from her and look at the male corpse to my left. He's much bigger than the woman, and his hips almost reach the edges of the table. I wouldn't be surprised if the table suddenly started groaning under his weight. He's naked as well, but there are no wounds or marks. He's still got both of his hands. No strangulation marks, either. Boring.

The next man isn't boring, however. Not at all. I look at his face, blink, look again, then swallow hard.

I've seen his photo often enough to recognise him.

It's Winston Kindler.

CHAPTER TEN

"You're supposed to be in the police's morgue," I tell the corpse, wiggling my finger at him. I walk around his table, checking him from all sides, but he completely matches the Winston Kindler I've read about. Same deep-set eyes, same bushy brows, same stubbly beard the same pepper grey colour as his short hair. Not pretty but also not ugly. Just a normal man who you wouldn't look at twice if you met him in the street.

Lily's words echo in my mind. Him looking so ordinary, that may have been precisely the point. If he was a Fang, it would have been the best weapon against being discovered. Nobody would ever suspect a friendly sweet shop owner from being involved in anything criminal.

"What did you do, Winston?" I whisper, looking at his face. Some people think the dead look peaceful, but that's rarely the case, unless funeral directors use makeup, baby powder and wires in the corpse's jaws. Mr Kindler doesn't look peaceful in the slightest.

I stare at his chest, at the gaping wounds inflicted on him. His brother had said that his death had been a violent one, but now that I'm confronted with the evidence, I see that it's an understatement. Winston was slaughtered. There are at least twenty cuts to his chest and belly, many of them deep gashes. White rib bones are shining through one of the largest wounds. No wonder he was found in a puddle of blood. He must have bled out fast.

I step even closer and analyse the cuts. Some of them are random, but hidden beneath the arbitrary crisscross pattern are three very precise cuts. They are the ones that killed him. Quickly, too. He was probably dead by the time the other wounds were inflicted on him. Almost as if someone wanted to make it look more violent than it was.

There are a few areas of the body that every assassin knows. The points of no return, my teachers used to call them. When you stab there, the mark dies. Simple. Not all of them are always easily accessible. My favourite one, the spot beneath the armpit where you can slash the axillary artery, is often protected by clothing, especially in winter (although nobody ever protects their armpits in a fight, so it's handy for those dirty moves that make you stand out from the crowd). There are even more effective stabbing targets than the armpit though. On a hunch, I lift Winston's head, examining his neck.

Bingo. A small, almost unnoticeable incision at the back

of his neck. The knife must have gone straight through the spinal cord. Instantly incapacitated, followed by a quick death. The attacker must have come from behind, stabbed Mr Kindler before he even knew what was happening, and then, to hide the fact that this was a professional hit, added the other stab wounds all over the chest. To get some blood for special effects. Two of the deep cuts on his upper body would have hit arteries, giving the assassin all the blood he needed to make it look dramatic and violent.

I'm almost jealous of the way this was done. It's neat and clever. Unless you know what you're looking for, this could easily be mistaken for an emotional killing, not the clean assassination that it was.

"Why?" I ask Winston. "Why did you have to die?"

Suddenly, a feeling of urgency runs through me, making my goose flesh rise, and it takes me a second to realise that it's coming from Storm. Shit. I've closed the door behind me, and I don't know if it's safe to open it. Is there someone on the other side that Storm tries to warn me about? Or do I still have time to slip out before they get close enough to see me?

I focus on the emotions I'm getting from Storm. It's not a clear message, not actual words or images, just an intention. What I'm feeling from her gives me the creeps.

Hide.

I look around, already knowing that there's no good place to hide. Everything is open and easily seen. No blind spots, no wardrobes or closets. Leaves the textbook hiding place, the one everyone always forgets about. Behind the door. Most people never look back when they enter a room. Even when they turn to exit, they rarely look at the spot behind the door.

With two large steps, I'm there, pressing myself against the wall. I steady my breathing, glad of my training that taught me how to control my entire body, including the way I breathe.

There's nothing I can do about the light still being on; there's no light switch anywhere to be seen. I'll just have to hope that they don't notice or at least don't suspect it's because someone's already in here. It could just be an electrical fault. I cling to that idiotic hope and wait.

The sound of someone walking down the steps makes me force my body to relax. When you're tense and in an uncomfortable position, you're more likely to make a sound and give yourself away. By relaxing, pretending that everything is fine, you trick your body into behaving, into not acting on the fear.

One day, I should really sneak into the Pack's lair and thank my teachers, especially Miss Joan. Then I'll kill her as revenge for all the things she did to me. She was a great teacher, but she liked to use role play in her lessons. Most of the time, I was playing the role of the mark. I got beaten up by her most days. Stabbed, occasionally. And worse. Shifters heal quickly, even when human, and they made full use of that.

I push the memories from my mind. This case is making me reminiscence far too much. I'll be glad when it's over, and I can go back to my normal day job. Night job. Whatever.

A key is pushed into the lock. Time slows down as I

focus all my senses on my surroundings. I need to be quiet, quick and qabalistic. The three Qs. I've always found the third one to be a bit forced, but I like it. Qabalistic: having a secret or hidden meaning. My whole life has been like that. Full of secrets, full of mysterious pasts and identities. In this case though, I'm just interested in the 'hidden' part of it. Namely, me staying hidden from whoever is about to enter the room.

The door opens. I continue to breathe normally. Quietly, but in a regular rhythm. If I hold my breath, I'll have to breathe faster and louder later on.

Heavy footsteps make me suspect that it's a man before I can even see him. When I do, I realise that I've underestimated his size. He's massive. His shaved head glistens in the cold light, his broad back looks like it belongs to an ox and his thighs... well, let's not get started on those. Tree trunks. That's what they are. He's two, maybe three heads taller than me and at least three times as wide. He could eat me for lunch and still demand dessert.

I smell the air. No, he's not a shifter. Thank the Great Cat in the Sky. He's just an extraordinarily large human. He walks to the corpse on the very left of the room, the one I hadn't looked at yet. Damn. Of course, he had to choose that one. It's not fair. Although, he could have taken Winston. That would have been even worse. Winston Kindler's body is my only good lead so far. Everything else is shrouded in secrets and questions, but him being here, not in the police's morgue, that's a big, fat hint. And this big, fat man is connected to it all.

I watch as he takes a knife from his pocket and

begins to saw off one of the corpse's fingers. Okay, he's definitely not the one who cut off the woman's hand and who killed Winston Kindler. He's making a mess of it. I could have done better as a toddler. At the end, he actually pulls at the finger to try and rip the last bit of skin apart, but it doesn't quite work, and he flays the wrist instead. Idiot.

When he finally manages to sever the finger from the poor man's hand, he wraps it in a piece of clingfilm and drops it in his pocket, along with the bloody knife. Ever heard of cleaning your tools after use? What a buffoon.

He turns back to the door. The moment of truth. Luckily, he never glances in my direction but keeps his eyes on the floor, as if he needs to concentrate where he's putting his massive feet. Well, if my shoes were the size of boats, I'd probably do the same. No running on rooftops for him.

I wait until the door closes behind him, then run over to the man's corpse. I scan his face, memorising his features, even though his skin has already started to blacken in places. He must have been here the longest, judging from the stadium of decay. He smells the worst, too. I wait another minute, then open the door.

Storm is waiting for me outside, her blue eyes glinting in the darkness.

"Let's follow him," I say, and she gives me a mental nod. I can almost see her smiling. Yes, cats love to hunt. I think Storm and I are going to have a good time together.

Half an hour later and quite a distance from the market square, both of us are sitting on a roof, watching the house on the other side of the road. We're in one of the wealthier parts of town. Not quite where the really posh people live, but close enough. Not a place I'd ever want to live. It must be a pain to keep the front gardens this neat and tidy.

The big man disappeared into the house a few minutes ago, but surprisingly, the house is still dark. Not a single light has been turned on. He did have a key though, so unless he stole it, he must be or know the owner.

Storm yawns and rubs her eyes with her furry paws. I try not to let her see how cute I find that. She'd probably kill me. Cats are everything but cute. Majestic, elegant, godly, but never, ever cute.

"You can go home," I whisper to her. "I can do this on my own."

She looks at me as if I'm crazy. She probably thinks of me as a helpless human. Well, she hasn't seen my panther yet. I shifted before I met her near the market, although I'm sure the other cats have told her about me. Besides, she can smell the cat in me. We recognise each other. So much so, that I sometimes have a crowd of male cats following me when I have my period. It's both embarrassing and adorable. Not that I'd ever be attracted to a male cat. My libido only works when I'm human, luckily. I don't even want to think about all the ethical implications of what a relationship with a cat would have. There are several things I'm proud to have on my police record. Bestiality wouldn't be one of them.

"Okay, stay," I mutter, keeping my eyes on the house. Not that anything is happening. It's as if the man simply went in there, lay down and fell asleep. Maybe that's precisely what he did, but it's a bit strange to cut off a finger before going to bed. No, my gut is telling me that something else is going on in that house. A secret meeting, maybe.

It's time to investigate.

"Warn me if someone's leaving the house," I tell Storm and she blinks at me lazily. I'm once again amazed at how blue her eyes are. It's like the sky met the sea in one enormous embrace while being sprinkled in glitter and starlight.

I slide down the roof, letting myself drop the last two metres to the ground. I land in a crouch, ready to jump into action should someone have heard me, but the street remains quiet. I assume that most houses here have intruder alarms, so people will be sleeping soundly, not knowing that most criminals see alarms as a welcome challenge.

I run over to the house until I'm back in the shadows, hunched beneath one of the large windows. The grass beneath me is wet even though it hasn't rained in days. They must be watering their garden. Such a waste of resources just to have greener grass than their neighbours.

I press my ear against the wall. There are definitely several people in there, some of them talking, but the walls are too thick for me to make out anything specific. I need to get closer. Annoyingly, with the shine of the street lamps, it's brighter out here than it is inside the house. Someone could be standing by the window, watching me, without me seeing them. No, looking through the windows isn't a good option. I need to get inside.

There's a balcony on the other side of the house that should be the perfect way to get inside. Or at least closer to the roof. I have a thing for rooftops.

Suddenly, there's a loud bang inside, like someone's been slammed against a wall. Shouts follow, indistinct but loud enough for me to separate them into four different voices. All men. Miss Joan's words pop into my head. *Crime is a men's world, girls. Better show them what you've got.*

Maybe I'll skip the roof after all. More loud noises inside, intermixed with groans and shouts, like they're having a brawl. Are they killing each other? Saves me from having to do the job, if they're indeed Winston Kindler's killers. Not that I'd mind...

I feel Storm's warning the same moment I instinctively swing around to a sound behind me. My knives are in my hands just in time to counter the first strike coming from the shadows. Someone is attacking me, but it's too dark to see his features. A man, judging from the way he moves and his size, but I know that looks can be deceiving. Another slash of silver and while I manage to block it, I don't see the tiny dart until it's too late.

It embeds itself in my throat, and a moment later, darkness overwhelms me. The last thing I feel is Storm's fear.

CHAPTER ELEVEN

The moment I return to consciousness, I swing my body into action, jumping up to face whoever is attacking me. Except that there's nobody to fight. I'm alone in a bright white room that's completely empty. Not even a window, just a metal door, sleek and shiny. Where the fuck am I?

I do a quick check of my situation. I'm tired and a little wobbly on my feet, but there doesn't seem to be any injuries or damage. My head is pounding. I push the pain away. I don't have time for a headache.

I feel for the dart that hit me on the neck, but it's no longer there. There's a tiny bit of dried blood where it must have been.

Annoyingly, I know exactly what I was poisoned with. The bitter taste in my mouth, the headache, the slight vertigo - I've experienced that many times during my training. Sweet Apple, called that because it smells that way when heated. Like a summer meadow full of apple trees and flowers. It's easy to make and very effective. It works instantly, causing the target to fall unconscious within seconds. Even better, it doesn't leave traces in the blood after the victim recovers. Or when they die. The only way to figure out if it was Sweet Apple is to recover the dart or to ask the victim about their symptoms. For something with such a pretty name, the aftertaste it leaves is disgusting.

I wish I had a glass of water, but for now, I'll have to do with spitting in a corner. It's not like this is my living room. Whoever brought me here will just have to deal with it.

I walk to the door, checking out the lock. It's modern but not impossible to crack. I have lockpicks sewn into my tunic - no, I don't. I groan. The poison must have affected me more than I thought. How did I not notice that I wasn't wearing my own clothes anymore?

They've put me in a simple t-shirt and tight-fitting trousers that are at least one size too small around the hips. I have no idea how they even managed to zip them up. Not what I'd usually wear, but at least I'm not naked. And yes, I'm trying very hard not to imagine how I was almost naked when they changed my clothes.

I check under my shirt. Luckily, I'm still wearing my bra. Which also means that I have a lockpick. I grin and pull it from under the wiring. I always count on the fact that people won't touch a woman's underwear if they search you. Unless they want to grope you, which usually ends with them dead or missing their balls. Either method works to keep them from doing it again.

I go on my knees and insert the picks into the lock. They're almost a little big for this kind of lock, but I'm sure I'll manage. I may not be as good as Benjamin, but there aren't many doors that will stay locked if I set my mind to it.

Just when I'm about to get the angle right, footsteps are coming from afar, moving towards me. Damn. I hastily push the lockpicks back into my bra and adjust my shirt, then get into position to attack whoever is about to enter my room.

"Are you awake?" a male voice asks from the other side of the door.

I hesitate for a moment, then reply with a sharp, "Yes."

"Stand back. I've got some hot tea and you don't want that all over you, should you try and tackle me."

I frown. Did he mention tea? As if we're going to have a little tea party in here? A relaxed chat with a steaming mug in our hands? I don't think so. Whoever he is, he attacked me, darted me and then kidnapped me. I'm not going to have tea with him. I'm going to make sure he's never going to drink tea ever again.

Still, when the key turns in the lock, I do step back and wait for him to enter. Of course, I'm planning to escape as soon as he takes his first step into the room, but when he does...

I gape at him.

"Lennox?"

He grins. "Nice to see you again, Kat. Sorry about the dart, I didn't recognise you in time."

I can't take my eyes off his face. Lennox. The only boy to ever escape the Pack. Besides me, of course, but I had help. Lennox. The boy who left me behind, left without saying goodbye.

I want to ask him how he got away, want to shout at him for leaving me, want to... but no words come.

He didn't lie about tea. He's carrying a large pot in one hand and two chipped mugs in the other. I could easily run right now. He wouldn't be able to stop me. But... Lennox. I need to know what happened to him. For a while, I was convinced he was dead until I heard a rumour about a white wolf being spotted outside the town. A white wolf with a black spot on his forehead.

He puts the pot and cups on the concrete floor and closes the door behind him. He doesn't lock it, which somehow makes me relax a little. He sits down on the floor, crosses his legs and begins to pour the tea as if this was the most normal situation possible.

I study him, mentally comparing him to the boy I knew. He'd always been tall, but now his bony frame has taken on muscles. His shoulders have become broad and his chest defined. The boy I knew has turned into a man.

He grins and runs his hand through his black hair. I never understood how he could have white fur as a wolf and pitch-black hair as a human. His bright blue eyes are the same though, no matter whether he's shifted or not. They're paler towards the centre and turn into an azure blue on the outside, before being ringed by the same black of his hair.

Now, there's a hint of black stubble on his cheeks and chin as well. Is he trying to grow a beard or did he simply forget to shave?

I force myself to look away from him and take one of the mugs instead, breathing in the scent of the steaming tea. It's good, surprisingly good. But then, he's a trained assassin. We school our senses, especially our sense of smell and taste. We wouldn't be able to work with poisons otherwise. In the end, tea is just another herb, except that it's used to make us feel good rather than to kill or injure.

"I forgot to bring milk, would you like some?" His voice reminds me of dark chocolate that's slowly melting in my mouth. I swallow hard. It must be a side effect of the Sweet Apple poison.

"No, thanks," I reply politely even though I prefer my tea with milk. I don't want to prolong this conversation, however. For some reason, he drugged and kidnapped me, and even though I want to know what he's done all these years, I want to know the reason for my abduction more urgently.

"Why am I here?" I ask while he calmly sips his tea. With his expensive black clothes, he looks almost posh. I have to hide a grin. That was our absolute nightmare when we were children. We never wanted to be posh. Rich, yes, although all that meant for us was never to be hungry and not to be beaten. But we didn't want to be all clever-sounding and well-dressed.

He smiles at me and makes me wait until he puts his mug down. "You were in the wrong place at the wrong time," he says, his eyes meeting mine. They're full of warmth, confusing me. "I'm sorry I had to dart you, but I couldn't risk alerting the people inside. They would have done much worse had they found you."

"You attacked me," I accuse him. "You could have killed me!"

He shrugs. "I didn't recognise you at first. You've changed a lot since I last saw you."

He gives me an appreciative glance, his eyes wandering up and down my body. It seems I've been not the only one checking the other out. Suddenly, I feel even more uncomfortable knowing that it was likely him who undressed me. Before, it was an unknown bad person, but now... This is all very confusing. Too emotional. I need to get myself under control. This isn't me, the child from back then who's happy to see her friend again. No, I'm Kat, the assassin, the owner of Meow, and he's someone who could threaten me doing my job.

"What were you doing there?" he asks me and I laugh darkly.

"You could have asked me before you poisoned me!"

"I already said I'm sorry," he replies, his voice still calm and measured. "I expected to be alone, and I panicked."

"What were you doing there?" I throw the question back at him.

He smiles. "I asked you first."

"Well, you're the one who needs to apologise, so you answer first." I can't help but grin. This almost feels like old times. We constantly argued but we rarely ever had proper fights.

Lennox sighs. "I was there to protect my current employer. He was having a meeting inside and asked me to keep an eye on the perimeter. I didn't really expect any trouble, but then I saw an intruder and had to act. When I realised it was you, I decided to bring you here rather than tell my boss. He doesn't know about you. Yet."

That last word hangs in the air, making a slight shiver run over my back.

"Who's your employer?" I ask warily.

He gazes down at his mug. "I can't tell you that. He's a very private man."

I snicker. Most criminals are. They're private people because they have things to hide. Skeletons in their closets, body parts in their fridges.

Lennox looks up again and meets my eyes. "Now it's your turn. What were you doing there? Did the Pack send you?"

I gape at him. "The Pack?" Of course, he doesn't know. How should he? I laugh. "No, I've got my own company now. I'd give you a business card, but they're in my bag. Which I no longer have." I frown at him in annoyance.

"Sorry, I'll give your stuff back to you once we're done here. But how can you be away from the Pack? Why would they let you go? You were always a thorn in their side, but you were one of their best assets."

His eyes wander to my neck, the place where a collar once sat.

"I had a bit of help," I admit. "I'm on my own now. I have my own team, my own base, my own morgue. And my own cases, one of which brought me to that house."

"But..." He's obviously confused. "The Pack

wouldn't just let you go. Even if you managed to escape, wouldn't they try to get you back?"

Suddenly, his expression hardens. "You're lying to me. You're still one of them." His voice turns bitter. "Here I am, being nice, giving you tea, hoping that we could maybe, I don't know, become friends again, while everything you say is a lie. They've trained you well."

I shake my head. "Look at me. I'm not lying to you. Yes, they tried to get me back. Yes, they almost succeeded. They caught me once, but I got away. Not before finding out one important thing, however: They can't put a collar back on an uncollared adult. Not after more than a day or two. It would kill me. So their choice was between killing me and letting me go."

He still looks at me suspiciously. "I know the Pack. They'd prefer killing you rather than let you set a precedent for others who might want to leave."

I snicker. "Everyone wants to leave. Except for the leadership, obviously. I don't think anyone wants to be in the Pack."

"I know a few people who loved being there," Lennox says. "It gave them a sense of community that they hadn't experienced before."

I laugh bitterly. "On the expense of those they bullied. But anyway, you're right. They would have killed me - if I hadn't provided them with an incentive not to."

"What?" he asks sharply.

"Money. Lots of it. The... friend... who helped me leave also gave me some money to start my business with. Instead of using it for that, I gave it to the Pack to leave me alone."

I've never told anyone that. The others at Meow believe I only got the house and maybe a modest sum, but I've not had the courage to admit to them that I've used the rest as a bribe.

"It must have been a lot," Lennox mutters. "A hell of a lot. Who's the friend who gave it to you?"

Good question. Wish I knew.

"Can't tell you," I quip. "You didn't tell me who your employer is, either."

He sighs. "Let's say I believe you. What did you do at the house last night?"

Last night? Have I been out that long? The room doesn't have any windows, and my watch has disappeared along with my other belongings.

"What time is it?" I ask.

He sighs again, impatience beginning to show in his eyes. "Half past nine in the morning. I can get us breakfast once you've finally told me why you were there."

"I'm investigating a murder case," I admit, but before I continue, he starts laughing.

"Investigating? Are you serious? You've switched sides?"

"Just this once," I say grudgingly. "The offer was too good to refuse."

He's still laughing. "I can't believe you're doing this. You, especially. You were always the best at killing."

I smile proudly. "You really think that?"

Lennox nods. "Yes, and you know that. Nobody else had your touch. They were either too brutal or too gentle. You simply went there, killed the mark and left. Cold as ice but I loved it."

A faint blush spreads over his cheeks, but it disappears quickly. "Who was murdered?"

I hesitate for a moment, not sure how much information I can give him. For all I know, he could work for the murderer. Or worse. He could be involved in the Fangs.

"No one special," I reply vaguely. "But I discovered a basement full of corpses while following a lead, which then, in turn, led me to the house last night. I'm sure there's a connection."

"You should stop there," he says quietly, staring at his mug. "The people I work for... they're dangerous. I'm not saying they're involved, but you don't want to get in trouble with them. Hell, you don't even want them to know that you exist." He pauses for a second, then takes a wallet out of his trouser pocket. "How much did your client offer you to solve the case? I can match it if you stop investigating."

I gape at him. "Are you trying to bribe me?"

"You just told me you bribed the Pack," he replies with a hollow chuckle. "How is this different?"

I jump up and glare at him. "Because I had to pay the Pack or they would have killed me. It was a matter of life or death. This... this is nothing like it."

He sighs. "Maybe it is, Kat. There is more to this than you know."

CHAPTER TWELVE

He looks up at me, a sad frown forming on his forehead.

"I can't."

"So you just want me to take your money and leave this case alone? Not find out who killed Winston Kindler? Not give his brother closure?"

His eyes widen. "What did you say?"

This time it's my turn to frown. "What of all that didn't you understand? I was saying no, basically."

"That name... Kindler?"

I sigh. "Yes, the name of the murder victim. Winston Kindler."

Suddenly, he smiles, confusing me. "That's got nothing to do with us. But I know who did it."

Standing outside in the cool morning air, I'm surprised by how quick that kidnapping was. I'd always imagined being imprisoned for days or weeks, tortured, forced to tell my kidnappers all my secrets - and here I am, talking to my former best friend, wearing my own clothes again and having had a lovely tea. Kidnapping has never been this nice.

"The people in the house last night weren't all part of the organisation I work for," Lennox explains. "I wouldn't be able to help you if one of us had done it, but the man responsible is already in our bad books. We were planning to get rid of him soon, so it's actually rather handy for you to want him. If you kill him, it won't be blamed on us. Just leave a calling card, and nobody will suspect that I helped you."

I grin. "Win-win. What organisation do you work for?"

I'd hoped to surprise him, but sadly, he's too well-trained.

"Nice try, but you know I can't tell you. I don't officially work for them anyway, but my boss does, so I'm involved but not on paper. It's better that way, I wouldn't want my name to appear on any of their files. Sometimes, it's better to stay in the shadows."

I huff. "Tell me about it. Life has become harder since I'm no longer working as an anonymous Pack assassin, but at the same time, I get to decide who to kill, so it's worked out better in the long run."

Lennox smiles at me. "Self-employment suits you. Do you get enough contracts to make it worth it?"

I nod. "I have to reject some of them because I don't have the time. Murder is in high demand, and I doubt that will ever change. And with the streams of refugees settling in the city, there's always more people filling the places of those who've died. Otherwise, I'd be scared that soon nobody would be left in this town but us assassins. By the way, do you still get to do that? Or does your master make you do other things?"

He shrugs, running a hand through his black hair. It shimmers in the sunlight, making it seem even more black than it already is. I wish I could touch it. No. I don't. What am I suddenly thinking?

"Sometimes," he says, distracting me from my inappropriate thoughts. "I do a lot of different jobs for him. It always depends on what he's working on. Sometimes, I still do freelance contracts for other people if I get the chance." He turns and looks around the deserted street. "We shouldn't stay here. Let's move and talk on the way."

I nod and follow him down the street and right into a narrow alleyway.

Suddenly, relief floods me, but it isn't my own. I stop and look around until I spot a black cat far above us on a roof. I smile at Storm and continue walking, glad to know my new friend kept watch on me. I'm sure she would have called the other cats for help should I have stayed away for longer. I've got a good feeling about Storm, like she's a kindred spirit. If I was just a cat, without this human side, I might be just like her.

"Everything alright?" Lennox asks, following my glance, but Storm has already disappeared.

"Yes," I mutter, not quite wanting to divulge my secret yet. I used to trust Lennox implicitly, but that's years ago, and right now, I don't even know who exactly he's working for. Worst case scenario, his boss is part of the Fangs or somehow connected to the Pack. The latter is unlikely, not with Lennox's history, but still. Better to keep some of my cards hidden until it's time to play them.

"Tell me about what happened," I ask, not just to distract him but also out of genuine interest. "You left me a note, you told me you'd come back for me, but you never did."

I try to keep the accusation out of my voice, but my twelve-year-old self has taken over, drenching me with the pain I felt back then. I shudder at the intensity of the emotion. I'd tried to forget how hard his disappearance hurt me. After Lennox, I never tried to befriend one of the other children. I'd lost him and I wasn't going to go through that anguish ever again. Only when Lily came along, that changed. She was the first person who I'd allowed into my locked heart as an adult. While I like Benjamin and Bethany, I love Lily. Not in a sexual way, but as a friend. She's become family, the first time I've ever really had that feeling. Well, except for when I had Lennox. He'd been like a brother. Now... I'm not sure what to call him, how to think of him. Friend? Acquaintance?

"... I didn't manage to, I'm sorry. I never forgot about you. I tried to get the funds to buy you from the Pack, but when I finally had the money they asked for, they took it all and laughed in my face. Then tried to kill me. I almost died, Kat. If my master hadn't found me, I'd be dead."

I stop walking, staring at him. "You tried to buy my freedom?"

He nods. I can almost see the dark memories that are making his brows draw together. He used to do that when he didn't want anyone to know that he was feeling sad.

"Yes, I did. But as I said, they betrayed me. I shouldn't have expected it to work, but I was both desperate and stupid. Somehow, I still had the hope that not everybody in the Pack was rotten to the core."

I laugh bitterly. "I would have been able to tell you that."

Lennox sighs. "I know. They always treated me differently from you. I always had more privileges, so I thought I could count on the same leniency again. I was wrong."

He rubs his abdomen.

"Did they stab you?" I ask, and he immediately removes his hand from his belly.

"Amongst other things. But as I said, I survived and have been working for my master ever since. He made me stop trying to get you out of there, but he promised that he would help me set you free once you were an adult and able to work for him."

I raise an eyebrow. "I guess that never happened?"

He looks to the ground. "No, it didn't."

We walk on in silence. He leads me through the crafters' quarter, but we avoid any of the busy streets where shops will be open by now.

"Where are we going?" I ask finally. I know where we are, and I have a few theories about where we're headed, but I don't like not being in control.

"Almost there," he replies. To my frustration, he doesn't expand on that.

"How did you escape?" I ask, unwilling to stay in

silence. He owes me that answer. I've been wondering for almost ten years how he managed to get away from the Pack. And why he didn't take me with him.

"Remember how they always told us that only those with special abilities could open our collars? And how they proved it by having us try it on each other?"

I nod, remembering it all too well. We couldn't even touch our own collars without pain shooting through our heads. They showed us that we could touch other children's collars without either of us feeling the pain, but none of us ever managed to open them.

"Well, that's only partially true. Actually, it's not true at all. It wasn't about abilities. The adults who opened the collars, they always did it with one hand only, remember?"

Again, I nod. It's not something that's struck me as strange before, but he's right. We even tried to copy them by touching it with only the fingers of our right hand, but it was useless. None of us ever managed to open a collar.

"That's because they were holding a key in their other hand," Lennox says, and I stop, staring at him.

"A key? They never used a key on the collar, there was no lock, just that clasp at the back."

He smiles grimly. "Not a key in the physical sense. It's an object that needs to be held so that the holder can open the collar. Not sure if it's some sort of magnet or electricity, or magic, but you need that key to open it. With the key, anybody can do it.

"So all you had to do was figure that out and steal a key," I whisper, the implications of it all rushing through my mind. All those children, they could all be freed. I never thought it possible because I believed in the special power bollocks, but now... so many possibilities.

Lennox nods. "I wasn't sure though, and I didn't want to endanger you in case I was wrong. I knew that if they caught me, I'd be dead. You understand why I had to try it on my own, right? I was always planning to come back for you in case it worked. But..." He sighs deeply. "Do you remember how it felt when your collar was taken off for the first time? The rush of adrenaline, the urge to shift, all your senses going in overdrive?"

"Yes, I do. The man who opened my collar, he helped me control it."

"Then you were luckier than I was," he says, sadness tinging his voice. "I shifted and went feral. I ran and ran and it took me hours to get back in control of my wolf. By the time I managed to shift back, I was far outside the city, far away from the Pack's lair. I knew they would have noticed my absence by now and that all the guards would have been briefed. Security would have been too tight to sneak in and get you, especially if they'd figured out that I knew about the collars."

"They had us sleep in the main hall," I say slowly, remembering how we were all ushered out of our dormitories without any explanation, even though I knew it was because of Lennox disappearing. At least he'd left me a note. Otherwise I would have thought he'd been killed by the Pack.

"There was no coming back for me. I never expected to see you again, I didn't even know if you were still alive. A few years ago, I sometimes came across your paws, but then that stopped."

"Yes, I didn't think there was any point in continuing it," I reply quietly. After Lennox ran away, I'd started leaving tiny paw print marks near corpses. Just in case. They were too unnoticeable for anyone other than an assassin who was looking for a calling card. Most of us have one. A way to show each other who made the kill. Mostly, to brag. In my case, it was a message to Lennox. Not that I ever got an answer. But now, it feels good to know that he sometimes saw them. It wasn't all for nothing. In some strange way, our friendship didn't end when he left. It kept on going through those small moments, like when he saw my marks or when I heard about the white wolf being spotted.

"I'm glad you didn't leave me there voluntarily," I say eventually. "It was hard without you."

He puts an arm around my shoulders, surprising me. We've not touched in any way since I woke up. No hug. Now, I regret that. I should have hugged him. Let's do it now. I turn and wrap my arms around his chest. Once again, I realise how broad he has become. It used to be easy to hug him; hell, I was able to link my hands on his back. Now, not even my fingertips touch as I try to embrace him like a tree trunk.

He hesitates for a moment, then he returns the hug, pressing me against his warm body. I breathe in his scent, that wild, untamed wolf scent mixed with masculine spices.

"It's good to have you back," he whispers, pulling me even closer. Our bodies are touching everywhere now, and I'm suddenly very aware of how we have changed. He's a man now, I'm a grown woman. I didn't have boobs when I last hugged him. Well, not very developed ones. Now, they're squeezed tight against his hard chest. Little tingles spread from my nipples through my body and hastily, I step back.

He releases me and silence falls, both of us a little embarrassed. And shocked, in my case. My body responded to him. Not like him as a friend, but as a man. That's something I will have to think about. Not that there's any chance of us being more than friends. We're both busy, I still don't know who he's working for and besides. We're assassins. We don't do relationships. We kill and get killed, simple as. And not only that. I'm a cat, he's a wolf. It's no coincidence that dogs and cats hate each other. It's something intrinsic, something that sometimes burst to the surface when Lennox and I were arguing. An animosity that couldn't be explained. A tension that wasn't supposed to be there. Can things like that overcome? I'm not sure.

"We should go," I mutter and wait for him to lead the way. He looks at me, but I evade his gaze, not wanting him to see how vulnerable I feel in this moment. I thought I had my emotions under control.

Damn, I was wrong.

CHAPTER THIRTEEN

We stop in front of a tall, narrow building squashed in between two broader houses like a piece of cheese between bread.

"We're here," Lennox says and fumbles in his pockets, probably looking for a key.

"What's here?" I ask, still frustrated by the fact that he's led me to goodness where and I don't have a clue about who we're going to see. It could be a trap.

"Patience, kitty," he chuckles. I almost hit him for using that old pet name. I'd forgotten that he used to call me that. He was the only one who was allowed. Barely. Sometimes, I did hit him for it.

He seems to know exactly what I'm thinking. "I assumed you were going to beat me," he laughs. "Glad to know I was wrong. Can I call you pussy cat now?"

I knee him in the balls. Not hard, I'm not that cruel, but hard enough to make him wince and bend over.

"Alright, lesson learned," he wheezes. "No pussy cat.

Now step back and wait out here while I check if he's there. He doesn't like being surprised."

I want to protest, but he shoots me one of his famous trust-me-don't-talk-back looks. I remember those, too. He was one of the few people I listened to. Well, one of the few who didn't need to use threats or violence to keep me under control.

While he unlocks the door and goes inside, I study the street. We're at the very edge of the city, close to the river. Old city walls surround this area, no longer guarded or used. They look pretty though, and I used to love running on top of them, imagining that I was a soldier protecting the city. I laugh to myself. Such a childish idea. Protecting the city. This town doesn't need protecting from outsiders, only from itself. From its people. I don't know if every city has such a high percentage of criminals or if it's just us. Most people I know are involved in some kind of shady business, whether it's forgery, theft or killing, but then, that doesn't say much. I don't really mix with ordinary people, unless it's to free them of life, obviously.

The street is mostly clean and the little front gardens are well looked after. This area isn't as posh as the one I went to last night, but it's still one of the better places to live. Not enough rich people to make it a target for thieves but also not cheap enough to attract the less wholesome parts of the population.

Lennox is taking his sweet time. I check my knives are all where they're supposed to be. My poison darts are still in my tunic collar. I have some other supplies in my bag, but I've certainly got enough weapons on me to defend myself. Or to attack. Either is a possibility in my line of work.

Meow.

A small cat is hiding behind a bush in the garden opposite.

"Hello," I whisper. "Are you one of Ryker's?"

Assent is projected towards me. Nice to know I've got another one of my spies on hand.

"Get some of your friends," I whisper, knowing the cat will hear me but nobody else will. "Explore the area. Check out this house. Watch if there's anything strange happening."

Meow.

Hunger. In response, my own stomach begins to growl a little.

"I'll make sure you get fed when I get back home," I promise. "All of you, however many of you there are."

The cat gives me one last look, then runs off, leaving me with a little more confidence about the current situation. Even if Lennox is hiding something, I will find out what's going on here. For him to offer me so much money, it must be something big. Something important.

A strange urge to protect Lennox creeps its way into my mind. I don't want him to come to harm. Then I remind myself that he's done very well for ten years without me protecting him, so it's rather ridiculous of me to think that he needs me. He's a grown man, he can look after himself. He'll know when to get involved and when to stay away.

"You can come in now!" he shouts from inside the house, and I gladly follow his voice. I hate waiting.

. . .

He's in the living room, together with a man who's got his back to me. I sniff the air. Something is familiar about this man, even though I can only see him from behind. His smell... I've met him before, but not long enough to properly remember his scent. Having a human mind and access to the senses of a panther means that I often get messages from them both, but I don't always have time to connect them. In this case, I know the scent, but I didn't get a chance to connect it to a memory. It happens to me a lot. Sometimes, I wonder if we're supposed to be like this. Shifters. Part human, part animal. Not quite either. Maybe we're really a mistake of nature, as some of the teachers at the Pack used to say. Not just an accident. A mistake. Something that can only be corrected by force.

"Meet my friend," Lennox says, a slight hesitation before the last word. Does that mean this is his boss, perhaps?

Slowly, the man turns around.

"Lovely to see you again," he says with a warm, pleasant voice. Fuck. It's the man in the top hat. My anonymous benefactor. The man who saved me.

When I first met him, he was wearing a hat and a waistcoat. Now, he's dressed in a simple but expensive suit. His hair is almost entirely white save for two black strands loosely pulled back. His eyes are just as intense as I remember. The scars on his cheekbones don't seem as pronounced now that I'm not in a dark room with him.

"You," I stutter, completely taken aback. I didn't expect this, not in the slightest. I only saw him once, all our communication since then has been by letter. Sometimes, he sent me details of jobs he wanted me to do - people he wanted me to kill - and once he even sent me a warning about the Pack being active in the area. In a way, I knew he was watching me from afar, but he never seemed interested in meeting me face to face again.

"You two know each other?" Lennox asks in confusion.

I nod, still rattled and a little confused. "He's-"

"A friend," the man interrupts. Shit, I don't even know his name. I never told Lennox about my mysterious benefactor, right? Did I? We talked about so many things, and I was so lost in memories...

"We've met before," he adds. "But why have you brought her here?"

Oh, so Lennox hasn't told him yet. What did they talk about while I was waiting outside? The weather? Cloudy with a chance of murder.

"She's investigating a murder case that involves Mr Kindler," Lennox says. "I thought you might have some information for her."

The man smiles. "Mr Kindler, yes, I heard about that. My granddaughter used to go to his shop a lot. Until the rumours started, then she stopped, obviously."

"What rumours?" I ask immediately.

"That his sweets contained certain substances," he replies smoothly. "Things you wouldn't want your child to eat."

"Like sugar," Lennox quips but it's clear the mystery man doesn't find it funny.

"Is that what this is all about?" I ask, realising the implications. "Someone killed Winston Kindler to stop him from doing that? Or for revenge?"

The man's eyes meet my own, unblinking, so intense. I make my panther rise to the surface, and for a moment, I know that my pupils change colour. His eyes widen, then he gives me a small smile.

"I know who killed him. I also can't tell you who did it because I support why they did it. All I can advise is that you stop investigating and leave these things alone."

I frown. "Are there going to be consequences if I continue?"

"Not from my side, no," he says, surprising me. "But you're walking on dangerous paths. There are people involved who you don't want to be noticed by, my dear. If I were you, I'd stay away from them. Especially with your history."

Until now, Lennox has stayed quiet, but now he asks, "What did he sell? What was in the sweets that would make someone want to kill him?"

The man turns to Lennox, his expression hard. "I shouldn't tell you this, but it may persuade our friend here to keep her nose out of it." He sighs deeply. "I don't need to tell you this, you already know how more and more shifters have been born over the past decade or so. Humans and shifters procreate, knowingly or not. Even if not all children are born shifters, they may carry the genes and pass them on to their offspring. Some people are scared of that. They want humans to stay pure.

They don't want evolution, they want control. Having the Pack is one way of them to keep a tight leash on shifters. Pardon the pun. But the problem with children is that they don't always shift until adolescence. There's no way of knowing whether they have the genes or not until then. So instead of waiting, someone has come up with a new way to make sure shifter children don't grow up into shifter adults."

"The sweets," Lennox gasps, echoing my thoughts. "They're poisoning them."

The man nods, a sad frown appearing on his forehead, making him look older. "They've found a poison that only affects children with shifter heritage. I don't know what it does. It doesn't seem to kill them outright, but maybe it will over time. Or maybe it will turn them infertile. Anyway, it's not something I would want my granddaughter to eat."

I nod. "Is she...?"

"Her mother. My daughter in law."

Now it makes sense. The reason why he helped me. The reason why he's telling me all this. He has shifters in his family, even though he isn't one himself. By helping me, and Lennox, he's trying to make this town a better place for his granddaughter.

"That's why you don't want me to investigate. Mr Kindler was one of the bad guys. He was trying to hurt shifters. Whoever killed him did something good. His killer is one of us."

"One of us?" Lennox snorts. "In this business, there are no bad and good guys. We're all bad, remember? We kill for money. When did that stop being bad?"

I shrug. "Technicalities. Just because I'm an assassin doesn't mean I can't have morals. I would never hurt a child or an animal. I don't like to torture my victims, unless they deserve it. I make it quick and painless. I'm basically a nice assassin."

Mystery man laughs, although there's still a certain sadness reflected in his eyes. "Nicely put. But you were not quite correct. Winston Kindler didn't have much choice in the matter. He was coerced into doing it by the same people who I regularly have to fight against. Something your young friend has been helping me with."

I look at Lennox, who seems a little uncomfortable with being called 'young'. I grin at him. I'm going to call him 'my young friend' a lot from now on. If there is a now. Will we stay together after this? Meet regularly? Or will this be our last meeting? Will we go our own ways, accepting that life has pulled us apart?

I think about everything I know by now. "The hand. It was a threat."

"Huh?" Lennox asks eloquently.

"I found a note in the sweet shop that led me to a flat near the market. They had a female hand in the fridge. I assume it was a message to Winston Kindler. He either knew the woman, or it was to tell him that this would happen to him should he not do what he was told." Then I remember another thing. "The note mentioned 100 children. Maybe that meant that Kindler was supposed to poison at least 100 children?"

I look at Lennox, realising something important. "I found four bodies yesterday, one of them was the woman whose hand had been cut off. A man came to that basement and I followed him to the house where you... where we met. That means the man will be involved in poisoning the children."

Lennox cringes. "He arrived about half an hour before I found you?"

I nod.

"Then he's untouchable. I know him. Nobody would ever dare to attack him. My employer works with him and even he is scared."

Interesting. That means mystery man isn't Lennox's boss. Then how do these two know each other?

"As I said. Leave it alone," the man says, giving me a grim frown. "Don't worry, things are being done about it. Go back to your business. I can provide you with some new marks, if you're bored."

I shake my head. I don't want his help. I don't need it. I have enough contracts to last me for months. But it doesn't feel right to just stop here. I'm so close. Now that I have this vital information, more and more things are beginning to make sense. Why all his sweets were given away for free after his death. What quicker way to distribute them to children from all across town than by basically throwing them at them. And Caitlin, the girl from the shop, maybe she's involved somehow. She said her family was poor; she'd be an easy target to bribe and manipulate. Perhaps she spied on Mr Kindler.

"And now I really must continue my work," the man says, making it very clear that this conversation is over. "Don't try finding me here again. I don't live here, and neither do I usually work here. If you need me, you know how to contact me, but keep it for emergencies. I don't want to hear about this Kindler affair again."

"Yes, sir," Lennox says and I nod. Maybe that nod is a lie, maybe it isn't. I haven't decided yet. I'm going to have to think about it all, at home, with the rest of Meow and with the cats.

CHAPTER FOURTEEN

I don't take Lennox home with me. It's still too fresh, and there's too much work to do. We're going to meet again tomorrow, though, to talk it all through. Without me being his kidnapping victim. We've chosen a neutral turf, a cafe in town, and we're going to have a lovely tea and maybe even some cake. And no, it's not a date. That's what I keep telling myself as I run back home, using the roofs as my street. Definitely not a date. I've known him since I was three or four, so no, how could it be a date? It's not like we've only just met.

I'm glad when I get back to the Meow headquarters and can fill my head with other thoughts. Lily and Beth are lounging in the living room.

"Benjamin is outside, feeding the cats," Lily greets me. "Where the fuck have you been?"

I shrug and throw myself onto one of the sofas. "I've been kidnapped. Nothing special. I also got lots of new information on this case. If anyone wants to hear it, you'll need to provide me with some food. I'm starving."

Beth throws a pack of crisps at me, and I lazily catch it with one hand.

"I was thinking of proper food, but this will do for now," I mutter, my mouth watering as I rip open the bag. I've not had anything to eat all day, and I'm famished.

"So, what was that about kidnapping?" Lily asks. "Who do I have to kill?"

"A boy from my past." I sigh. "Man, actually."

Lily whistles. "Is he hot?"

"If Kat has noticed that he's a man, he must be," Beth grins. "Tell us all about it."

Since when has Meow turned into a horde of gossiping women? We're never this relaxed and we certainly don't talk about boys. Men. Whatever. The opposite sex.

"I know why Winston Kindler was killed," I begin but Bethany interrupts me.

"Boooring! Tell us about your lover!"

I groan, hiding my face behind the crisp bag. "He's not my lover. I shouldn't have mentioned him. He's just a guy who kidnapped me and then had tea with me and then let me go."

Lily laughs. "Are you letting him kidnap you again?"

"No," I snap. "I'm not into kidnapping. But I am going to meet him again tomorrow. To talk about the case."

"Suuuure," Beth chuckles, drawing the word out like chewing gum. "Just about the case. Then I'm sure you don't mind if we join you?"

What have I done to deserve this? I thought I was

the boss, but it seems I've now been turned into a... well, a what exactly? Woman to gossip about? A friend? I'd not anticipated that.

Luckily, Benjamin saves me by entering the room, his black jumper covered in cat hair. He has a cheesy grin spread across his face. He must have been spending a lot of time with the cats. I'm glad. I'd felt a little guilty about not being there to feed them. After talking to my humans, I'm going to have a chat with the cats, see if they've found out anything new. And tell them to spy on both the house I met mystery man in and on Lennox. Just in case.

"What have I missed?" Benjamin asks, leaning against the doorframe. Seeing him like this, it's easy to compare his boyish frame to Lennox's masculine body. I've been honest with Lily when I said that Ben is far too young for me. He's still a kitten, in a way. He doesn't even have a beard yet.

"Kat's got a boyfriend," Lily replies immediately, and I throw a cushion at her. Sadly, her reflexes are almost as good as mine, and she catches it before it can hit her.

"Winston Kindler poisoned children," I snap before this can get even worse. Immediately, I have the silence I wanted.

"What?" Beth asks, her smile gone. "How?"

I give them a quick summary of what mystery man told me.

"So that's why he didn't have to pay his bills in full," Benjamin mutters, taking a seat next to Beth. "And why he was getting extra payments. They were either bribes or to pay for the materials needed for the poison."

I nod. "It all fits together. Finally, most of our findings make sense. My biggest question though is whether he wanted to do it or whether he was coerced. Or whether he started as a supporter of the idea but then changed his mind, and to stop him from defecting, they threatened him."

"Cutting off a dead woman's hand is a rather intense way of threatening someone," Beth says, more serious than I've ever seen her. "But there are some questions that haven't been answered yet."

"Why don't you summarise," Lily suggests, and I nod in agreement.

Bethany seems almost surprised that we're both encouraging her, but then clears her throat. "Well, we don't know who slept in the storeroom at the sweet shop. You have some keys we haven't found locks to yet. Same with the number you found in Kindler's shed. And what about the Fangs? Are they the ones who came up with the poisoning? Are they the ones pulling the strings? Or is there a different connection to them?"

"All very valid points," I say, and she smiles. "The question is, are we going to continue investigating? I know none of you is a shifter, so maybe you have a different opinion on this, but-"

"They need to be stopped," Lily interrupts me. "We can't let people like that continue. Killing adults, sign me up, but poisoning children, doing who knows to their health? No, that's just wrong. I may not have a moral compass, but I do have a heart."

I smile at her. That's exactly how I feel. There are

some things that cross a line even assassins like us wouldn't cross.

"The man you met told you that he's working against them, right?" Benjamin asks, and I nod. "Then maybe we should switch sides. Stop investigating Kindler's murder. Stop treating him as the victim, and start looking for the killer not as someone to fight, but to ally with. They killed Kindler because of what he's done. That means they're against it and are on our side."

"Unless," I interject, "it was his own allies who killed him. The way he was stabbed, it was quick and efficient. The way you'd do it if you were either a professional, if you didn't have any emotional attachment to them or if you wanted to make it quick because you knew them. We can't assume that his killer was trying to stop the poisoning. Maybe Winston had become a liability and needed to be stopped before he told someone about what he was doing."

"Basically, we still need to find the killer," Lily sighs. "And then decide whether to kill them or work with them. Which means we're not really that much further at all."

I shake my head. "No, we've made a lot of progress. We have new angles to look at. Benjamin, I'd like you to find out who's bought the sweet shop. Maybe they're part of it, maybe they're going to continue the poisoning. Beth, you take a look at the powder I brought home from the market place flat. Maybe you can find out how exactly it works and if there's an antidote."

"I've already started while you had fun getting

kidnapped," she tells me with a small smile. "It's nothing that I've come across before. I'm going to have to borrow some books from friends to see if I can find anything mentioned."

"Friends?" Lily teases. "Since when do you have friends?"

"I have more than you," Beth snaps. "I've actually got a social life."

I want to laugh, but to be honest, Beth doesn't deserve to be teased. I don't know much about her previous life, but nobody here at Meow has had it easy. If she has friends, good for her. I wish the rest of us had, too. Especially Benjamin. He could do with some social interaction. I grimace mentally. Am I becoming a mother cat, making sure all my employees have a good work-life balance? Not really what you'd expect in a business that has the tag line 'We kill so you don't have to'.

"Lily, have you met Winston's brother yet?"

"No, but I have a date with him tonight." She winks at me.

"Well, I better let you get ready for that. I need some sleep."

Before I go to bed, I walk outside, looking for cats. One particularly large male cat sits on our front step as if he's waiting for me. His dark grey fur is bushy and soft, especially around his neck. It almost looks like a lion's mane there, slightly silver and shimmering in the evening light. His eyes are a deep yellow with thin, sharp pupils. His front paws are disproportionally large. I bet he can pack quite a punch with those.

He's not moving at all, except for his ears that flick left and right from time to time. There's a certain authority in the way he sits and stares at me.

"Ryker?" I ask, suspecting that this may be the leader of the cats. He certainly looks like a boss.

He blinks. I take that as a yes.

"Do you want to talk?"

Another blink.

"Alright, meet me in the backyard. I'll shift there, this is too exposed."

He walks away without a backward glance. What an arrogant beast. No wonder he commands an entire group of cats.

I go back inside and out again through the back door, shifting as soon as I'm outside. I shake my body, relaxing into my new shape. My fur immediately warms under the evening sun, and I'm tempted to lie down for a little nap. Sadly, there's work to do. As always.

Ryker jumps from the top of the yard wall, landing elegantly in front of me.

"Good evening," he says in a deep, posh voice. I'd expected him to either sound really rough or really posh, so it fits.

"Evening. Good to finally meet you."

"Likewise. My brothers and sisters have told me a lot about you. I've been curious about this human-cat they've been talking about."

"Brothers and sisters? Is that what you call them?"

He smiles, exposing his sharp canines. "We're a family. With me in charge, obviously. Every family needs someone to lead them. But yes, we belong together. We look after each other, help when one of us needs assistance, share our food if we need to. It started a couple of years ago when that cat murderer was haunting our streets. By sticking together, we had more of a chance to survive. And kill him."

I growl in surprise. "You killed a man?"

"Of course. He was a threat to catkind. You kill people too, don't you?"

"Yes, but..."

I don't quite know what to say. It's a bit disturbing to think that a couple of cats actually killed a human. Of course, I don't blame them if he'd murdered cats; in fact, I applaud them. But still... this is unexpected. And it might come in handy. If they've killed before, maybe they can do it again. Perhaps I could make them a permanent part of Meow. Not just spying for me, but doing the occasional assassination as well.

"Anyway, you wanted to talk to me?"

Ryker nods. "Storm told me that you got in trouble last night. I've got some cats on the case. They're surveying the house you were held in as well as the two humans you met afterwards."

This guy is amazing!

"I was about to ask whether you could do that for me," I admit. "Thanks for being so helpful."

His eyes twinkle with mirth. "It comes at a price. We need more food. Also, we have two orphaned kittens that need milk and warm blankets."

"That's a big request," I say, totally bluffing. I'll give them as much food as they want to, not just because they're helping me, but because they are cats. Simple. I'd much rather spoil some cats than humans. "What do I get in return?"

His smile disappears. "As much information as we can gather. Protection in case you get in trouble again. We should arrange some signals we can give your fellow humans, so they know what's happening." "You know, I don't usually get kidnapped," I protest. "That was a one-off."

"Call it part of the service. One scratch to say that you're hurt, two that you're taken, three that you're dead?"

I growl at him. "They won't appreciate being scratched. Besides, I'm not planning to die anytime soon."

"One day, we all need to die," he says calmly. A philosophical cat, seriously?

"Have you found out anything else that would be helpful?" I ask him to dispel the suddenly rather sombre mood.

"The human female working in the sweet-smelling shop. She sleeps in the shop, in the other room."

"In the storage room? On that mattress?"

"Yes. She's also been to visit a certain house near the market. The one Storm led you to."

"When?" I ask, my mind spinning. Caitlin is working with the people who may have killed her employer! I knew there was something off about her.

"Not long after you went there. Sadly, my brother had to go back to his kittens, so he wasn't able to follow her afterwards. She was back at the shop this morning though."

"That's helpful, thanks. I'll have another chat with her. Anything else?"

"That house no longer smells like death. I assume the dead humans have been removed."

Damn it. To be honest, I kind of excepted that, but it's still annoying. I was hoping I'd get another chance to examine Winston Kindler or the woman with the cut-off hand. At least we have the hand. That has to be good for something.

"Good, let me know if you find any other suspicious things or if one of the people you're watching do something strange."

"Like ripping off some flowers at a graveyard?" he asks with a grin. "Because that's what I saw the young male do."

He jumps off with a chuckle. I really hope that was just a joke. Really, really hope.

CHAPTER FIFTEEN

Yuck. Lennox has seriously brought flowers to our meeting. Does he assume that this is a date? It's nothing of the sort. This is a business meeting, a chat between old friends about an ongoing case. Nothing else.

I stare at his outstretched hand. If I take the flowers, does that mean some kind of commitment? Should I just take them now and feed them to some animal later on? And if I don't take them, will he be less likely to tell me about his employer? I need him on my side. I don't think flowers have ever been this important.

The only thing I've ever used flowers for is to rip off their petals in order to decide whether to kill or maim.

I decide to bite the bullet and take the flowers, looking at them with distaste. There's a glass of water on the table, so I drop them in there, planning to accidentally forget them when I leave.

"I still can't believe I found you again," Lennox says with a smile once we've sat down. It's a small, pleasant little cafe by the river. I've never been here before - I'm not someone who sits down in cafes with a book and a piece of cake - but I can see why Lennox chose this location to meet. We order our drinks from a waitress who's decidedly too cheerful, and as an afterthought, Lennox orders a plate of nibbles as well. Apparently, those are good here.

"It's not like you found me," I reply to his earlier statement. "We kind of crashed into each other by mistake."

He shrugs. "Yes, but it makes me happy nonetheless. You can't even imagine how often I thought of you. How often I was tempted to break into the Pack's headquarters and get you out of there."

"Well, I did get out, eventually. Let's not dwell on the Pack. I've gladly forgotten all about that time."

Lennox nods. "Me too. One day, when I'm rich and powerful, I'm going to shut them down. Free all the kids, then dismember the Pack leaders one by one."

"Can I help?" I ask with a grin. "That's pretty much what I've been planning for years."

He winks at me. "Together. Just like old times. They won't know what hit them."

The waitress returns and puts a steaming mug of tea in front of me. The colour is a little murky, like the water she used wasn't clean, but to be honest, I couldn't care less. I'm not here to enjoy my tea. I'm here to talk to Lennox.

"I've thought about yesterday," I say as soon as the girl has disappeared again. "I don't want to stop my investigation. Not because I want to punish or kill whoever murdered Winston Kindler, but because I want to help those kids. I can't stand by and watch children being poisoned. Children like us. Shifters." I sigh. "I spend so much time planning other people's death, and I don't have a problem with them suffering a little. But children, that's an entirely different matter. Imagine if it had been us. If we'd not been with the Pack."

He stares at me, his eyes hard. "I get what you're talking about, but you were told not to. It's too dangerous."

I sigh. "And when have I ever done what someone tells me to? This is important, Lennox. It's okay if you don't want to help, if you don't want to get involved. But please tell me who your employer is. Who was at that house when you caught me? They're involved with the poisonings, and I need to stop them."

He smiles sadly. "I can't tell you about my employer, but-"

"You're a coward," I huff.

Suddenly, he growls. His eyes turn bright yellow and goosebumps appear on his skin. The cafe around us goes quiet for a moment, but as soon as people realise that it was probably just a dog, they continue talking.

"Don't interrupt me," he snaps. "I was about to say that while I can't tell you about him, I can talk about the others. And that I've already started enquiries. I know you may not think the best of me, but I do have a heart, Kat. I can't see those children hurt either."

I stare at him. "You're going to help?"

He nods, a small smile appearing on his gorgeous lips. Wait, not gorgeous. Just... lips. If he's going to get involved, this has to stay strictly professional. I can't afford to develop feelings for him.

"I wanted to see what you were going to do. If you were going to drop it," he admits. "I was sure you wouldn't, but a lot of time has passed since we last saw each other. You could have changed."

"I *have* changed," I say softly. "I'm no longer the Kat you knew. That Kat has long since died, buried somewhere with the Pack."

He shakes his head. "No, you're still there. I know you like to pretend to be cold and heartless, but there's a conscience hiding deep beneath all your bravado. Compassion. That hasn't changed, and I doubt it ever will. They didn't manage to break you back then, which means nobody will ever manage that now."

I mull over his words. I don't think he's right. I've changed so much. I've become a lot colder than he realises. He only just met me yesterday. He doesn't know all that's happened. He has no idea of all the things I've done, things I've had to. Things that I'm proud of.

I take a sip of my tea and almost spit it out again. "That's disgusting."

He laughs. "I don't come here because of the quality of the tea. Wait until we get the food. That far outweighs the downsides of them using river water for their hot drinks."

I put my cup down, glaring at it. "River water? And we paid for that?"

Sure, I used to drink the dirty water in the river when I didn't have any other choice, but this is a cafe, not some kind of dump.

As if to prove his words, the waitress puts a large plate on the table, filled with all sorts of finger foods. Tiny meatballs, breadsticks, sausage rolls, cheese with grapes on cocktail sticks, some stuffed olives. It looks surprisingly good.

"Be sure to try the pickled aubergine," Lennox says and already reaches for some. "It's delicious."

I laugh. "You've become posh. You'd never have called an eggplant an aubergine in the past."

He shrugs. "It sounds nicer. Eggplant, who even came up with that? An egg growing on a plant? A plant that tastes like egg? It just sounds disgusting. Now, aubergine, that already sounds like a tangy taste that melts in your mouth with a certain sweetness."

I snort loudly. An elderly woman at the table next to us stares at me, but I just give her a smile. My table manners only go as far as sitting on a chair and not using my feet to eat.

We eat in silence for a moment. Lennox is right, the pickled eggplant is delicious. Never had anything like it before. It's not really something I'd buy.

"What do you know about the person who killed your sweet shop owner?" he asks suddenly. I spit out an olive pit and wonder how much I should tell him. Can I trust him? I once did completely, but now, I'm not so sure. I also feel protective of my case. It's my first murder case, after all. And my last. I'm never going to investigate a crime ever again. It's so much more fun to be on the other side of the law.

"They're a professional," I say after a moment. "Made Winston Kindler's death look like a violent, impulsive attack but in fact, it was a quick assassination. It was also very efficient and mostly painless, leading me to think that he didn't want his mark to suffer."

"Do you think the assassin was sent by Kindler's employers? The ones who gave him the sweets? Or by someone who figured out what he was doing and wanted to stop him?"

"It could be either," I admit. "Mr Kindler was threatened, maybe blackmailed. At the same time, he also made a good profit by selling those poisoned sweets, and there's no evidence that he'd stopped selling them. Now that I know about what that poison does, I'm beginning to think that the killer may be on our side."

"Our side?" Lennox repeats. "You think there are sides?"

I shrug. "Whoever is organising this hates shifters. We are shifters. Therefore, there are two different sides at the very least."

"True. And to be honest, I'm rather glad we're on the same side."

He gives me a disarming smile that makes me want to draw my knives and slit his throat. Not because I don't like him. Because I'm scared that I might fall for his charm. Not just because he's gorgeous, but because of all the good memories his presence conjures. I'd forgotten that there had been good times at the Pack. Times with Lennox hiding from our masters. Testing how much we could get away with before getting tortured. The smiles we'd give each other after our punishments, the gestures that meant we weren't giving in. We felt so strong back then. Invincible. When he left,

I was suddenly a lot weaker. At least I felt that way. It took months to build up my confidence again, and my masters took full advantage of that.

A shiver runs over my back at the memory. Lennox looks at me knowingly.

"Do you ever get nightmares?" he asks softly.

I glare at him. "Let's not get sentimental. We're here to talk about our mission."

He winks. Actually winks. Holy knives. "Are we?"

I growl. "Yes, we are. What are we going to do next?"

"The other men who were in the house. I can get us to at least two of them. Not sure we can get them to talk without killing them, though, and my master would not appreciate losing his business partners."

"Torture?" I ask with a grin.

Lennox shakes his head. "No, let's try searching their homes first. Maybe we'll find enough clues without talking to them."

"I can have my associates shadow them," I suggest. "They're very good at that."

He laughs. "Associates? My, you really have changed. Back when we were kids, I had to persuade you to let me help you. Now, you actually work with people? Voluntarily?"

I swallow a laugh. If only he knew about my cats. Maybe I'll tell him one day, once I know I can trust him. For now, I keep my cards close to my chest.

"Good, let's go," I say, ignoring his question as well as the plate of nibbles that is still half full.

"Already?" He looks a little disappointed for a

second, but he quickly smooths his expression. "I'd hoped we could talk for a bit more."

I sigh. "What do you want to talk about? Is it more important than children being poisoned?"

"Probably not." He grimaces. "You've always had a way with words. The power of persuasion."

I can't help but laugh. "That's because I'm right."

He looks at the nibble plate with a wistful glance, then simply shoves all the food into his bag. "Dinner," he says with a shrug. "I don't think I have anything left in my fridge."

I think of my own. Hopefully, Lily has put that bloody head into the cooling room. Not because I mind having a body part next to my food, but because it took up space that I could have used for junk food.

"Which one do you want to go to first? The fat or the thin one?"

I laugh, startling myself. I don't think I've ever laughed this much in a single hour. Lennox is doing something to me, and I'm not sure I like it. It scares me, to be honest.

"The fat one," I reply. "Does he have a name?"

"Not one you'll get to hear. My master wouldn't appreciate it, and as long as I'm in his employ, I better follow his rules."

I'm *so* glad I'm self-employed.

CHAPTER SIXTEEN

A kitten is following us. Not one I've seen before, but the way she looks at me makes it clear that she's one of Ryker's. I'm beginning to think that Ryker isn't just spying on my targets, but on me as well. Clever cat.

Lennox leads me across town to the same quarter where the house is that he knocked me out at. We pass it, and Lennox seems to think the same thing as me.

"Sorry. I won't do it again."

"You better not," I snap, but I'm smiling. "Or I'll have to seek revenge. You don't want to be faced with an angry Kat."

He laughs. "No, I really don't, I remember your temper tantrums. But we better leave the streets, we're getting close."

A moment later, we're on the roofs, jumping from house to house. Lennox occasionally does backflips and cartwheels that really aren't necessary. Show-off. It would be better if he crouched a little, like me, to stay hidden from any curious eyes. Not many people look up at roofs, but still, there's always the chance that someone may.

Finally, he stops on a dark red roof overlooking a garden pond with solitary duck swimming on it. The bird looks depressed. Poor thing. Maybe it can be a snack for the cats. That way, it's not been a waste of space all its life.

"Over there," Lennox whispers. "The brick house, that's his." He sniffs the air, his eyes turning yellow for a moment. "Nobody in. Let's do a bit of breaking and entering."

I return his grin and together, we jump off the roof and land in a crouch side by side. Just like old times. He keeps a look out while I pick the lock. Instinctively we've taken on our old roles, becoming a well-trained team again, despite all the time apart.

As soon as we step into the house, it's clear that the owner is very wealthy and likes to portray his wealth openly. Antique vases, oil paintings, expensive rugs. It all reeks of money. Lennox goes to disable the alarm system; he knows where it is because he's been here before. I begin to look around, a bitter taste developing in my mouth. Part of this wealth is connected to poisoning children. As much as I can understand and enjoy killing and poisoning adults, harming children is a step too far.

Besides all the opulence, there isn't much interesting to find in this house. The man seems to live alone. No family pictures, no women's clothes. A very badly stocked kitchen. He doesn't seem to spend a lot of time here, yet compared to Mr Kindler's house, this is a home that's actually gets lived in. His bed sheets are crumpled, and there are traces of body fluids on there that I don't really want to identify. I could give them a sniff, and my cat senses would immediately find out what they are, but no thanks. There are traces of drugs on his bedside table as well as some cigarette butts in an ashtray. I don't like people who smoke in bed. It makes their corpses smell like smoke.

"I found something!" Lennox calls from downstairs and with one last look around the bedroom, I join him in the hallway. He's shifted a large ornate mirror to one side, revealing a door behind it. I feel like I should have spotted that earlier, but I hadn't even started looking at the hallway yet. I was busy with the upper floor. Still, I'm a little annoyed that he found it and not me.

"Finally something fun," I mutter, then tell him how Winston Kindler's house was as boring as fuck.

"I do like a secret basement," Lennox says with a wide grin. One that likely mirrors my own. Hidden rooms are the best. I wonder what we'll find. Skeletons? Drugs? A sex dungeon? I've seen it all.

I go down first, not bothering with a torch. My cat eyes are good enough for this. Lennox can see in the dark too, but not as well as me. Poor doggy.

Down below, the air is musty and damp. I switch on the lights to expose a poorly painted room, with brickwork showing through some of the holes in the paint. Compared to the beautiful interior upstairs, this is a travesty.

In the centre of the room is a single chair made

from iron, complete with manacles and an iron collar. Lovely. Seems like the man uses this for interrogations or torture. Killing, maybe? Could be all three. A drain just beneath the chair shows that someone thought about what this room would be used for when they built it. It's handy to have a drain, saves having to clean all the blood from the floor. I know what I'm talking about. Sadly, most of my marks don't plan their assassinations in advance, which leaves me with having to make their deaths as bloodless as possible, unless I want to send a message.

"Nice," Lennox mutters appreciatively. A man after my own heart. "Can you smell that?"

I sniff the air. "The powder. The poison they're using on the kids."

He nods. "Let's find it."

There aren't many places it could be hidden. A few shelves line the walls, and two large metal boxes wait in the corners. I open one of them. It's full of torture equipment. My, that's quite a collection. I only have about half of what they have in here, and I'm a bit of a professional. Granted, I don't specialise in torture per se, but I am a little jealous. Something catches my eye behind the box, and I shove it to one side.

"Ha!" I exclaim before I can stop myself.

"What?" Lennox calls from the other side of the room. He's rummaging through the other box.

"There's another hidden door," I reply cheerily. "Let's see what's hidden behind it. Why would you put a secret door in an already secret room? Bit paranoid, don't you think?"

He comes over and stands close to me. I can feel his body heat on my skin, almost as if he's touching me. I both want to jump away from him and move closer. I decide for crouching low and climbing through the hole in the wall into the secret room. It's dark and smells of something very familiar. Blood. Human blood.

What the fuck have we got ourselves into?

I let my eyes adjust to the darkness and blink a couple of times. It's more of a tunnel than a room, leading away from the house. It must lead under the front garden and then across the road. Is this tunnel going to connect with the house opposite? Now that would be an interesting twist, but it wouldn't explain the scent of blood that's drenching the walls.

I move forward, my head almost touching the ceiling even though I'm crawling. Whoever built this wasn't a very big person. Definitely not the man I saw back at the basement where Mr Kindler now lies dead and abandoned. This was either done before he moved in here, or not for his use.

"See anything?" Lennox shouts from behind me.

"Not yet! This tunnel is very long!"

I hurry up, crawling on all fours over the luckily smooth floor. This isn't a quickly dug dirt tunnel, no, someone's put a lot of effort into it. It would almost be clean if it weren't for occasional blood stains on the walls and ceiling.

Finally, there's a light at the end of the tunnel. Literally, but I hope it might be a metaphor as well. I really need to find some solid evidence of whatever's going on here. Preferably a written confession that explains it all, so I can go back to my day job. This is too much work. Too many unknown variables. Not the way I like to do things. When I go on a job, I plan everything. It's rare that something goes wrong. With this case though, nothing is as it's supposed to be. I'm stumbling in the dark, and the more I search, the more questions I find. It's getting frustrating. Finding Lennox was a nice distraction, but I really want it to end.

I climb out of the tunnel and into a dark room. My cat eyes let me see enough to know that it's a lab of some sort. Much more expansive than the pieces of apparatus I found in that flat near the market. This is any scientist's wet dream come true. The shelves and cabinets lining the walls are well stocked with chemicals, glass jars and boxes. There are tons of supplies on the four long tables as well as long as equipment like Bunsen burners and stacks of test tube racks. All of it is extremely clean. It even smells of vinegar and cleaning supplies. I doubt I'll find much here. But why keep this lab so clean and then not remove the blood stains in the tunnel?

The tunnel entrance isn't barred like in the house I've just come from, but clearly visible between a desk and a filing cabinet. On the wall opposite is a thick metal door. I check it tentatively, but it's locked. There's nobody in the house, so I'll pick it later to look around whatever this house is. First, let's see if there's something useful here in the lab.

Lennox crawls out of the tunnel, jumping out not quite as elegantly as I did. Well, he's not a cat. That makes a big difference.

"Nice," he mutters appreciatively.

"Still like poisons?" I ask him and he nods.

"I've got my own lab, but it's nowhere as big as this. I could get used to having access to a facility like this. Maybe we can take it over once we've disposed of whoever owns it? Spoils of war?"

I laugh. "I like the way you think. As long as I get any knives that might be hidden somewhere."

"You've always had an eye for sharp things," he replies with a wink. "It really stank of death in that tunnel. Have you found any bodies yet?"

"No, but I've not opened any cabinets yet. It doesn't smell dead in here though."

He sniffs the air, his eyes turning yellow. The one thing I actually admit to is that wolves have a better sense of smell than cats. That's the only thing they're better at though. We win in everything else.

"There's something strange coming from over there," he mutters and slowly walks towards one of the closed cabinets. His eyes remain yellow, making him look kind of kick-arse. No, I did not just say that. It makes him look like a wolf-man. Not exotic. Not attractive in a strange way. Not at all.

I follow him, smelling the air. When I get closer, I can sense he's right. It's not the scent of death and decay that I smelled before, but something different. It feels familiar, but I can't quite put my finger on it.

Lennox carefully opens the wooden doors and steps back with a muffled sound.

"What is it?" I squeeze past him to see what's upset him.

Oh my. It's a row of jars with bits swimming in them. Organs. Body parts. But they're not big enough to belong to adults. No. Those are the organs of dead children.

"Bastards," I curse, looking at Lennox's shocked expression. "How can they do that?"

He just stares at me.

I let him be and take one of the jars, trying not to look at the small human heart. There's a label on it.

Wolf shifter.
Female.
8 years old.
Test 34 (2).
Deceased after 12 days.

My stomach roils. An eight-year-old girl. Murdered. Dissected. Given some sort of poison in a test. That's what it has to be about. The poison in the sweets. They must have tried it on children before they put it into mass production.

I'm going to find and kill them. Painfully.

"I wonder where they got the children from," Lennox says quietly, his voice made of ice.

He's right. It's not like there are many stray shifters running about. Most of them - well, almost all of them - are part of the Pack, controlled and enslaved. If Test 34 means that she was the thirty-fourth child to be given the poison, that would mean a lot more children falling victim to these monsters. There can't be more than a handful of stray shifters in the town, if even that.

Maybe none at all. No, they must have come from the Pack.

"I'm going to kill them," Lennox hisses. "They've been selling children for experimentation. I knew the Pack was bad, but I didn't expect them to be this unscrupulous."

Tears are threatening to destroy my last semblance of composure, so I turn away from him and randomly choose one of the shelves.

"Let's see if we can find more evidence. There must be a paper trail. Something that will tell us who's involved."

He mutters something but then copies me, taking apart the laboratory one shelf at a time. We're going to destroy them, even if we have to kill every single Pack member in town.

CHAPTER SEVENTEEN

When I get home, I don't bother stopping by the common areas. I don't want to see anyone. I need time alone to think and process what I've seen. I doubt I've ever been this shocked in all my life.

I let myself fall onto my hammock and stretch my legs. It feels good to be in my little sanctuary. My place of peace. Death and anguish don't follow me in here. This is my home and woe all who try to defile it.

"You look tired."

I jump up, grabbing some knives from my belt in mid-air, ready to throw them at the stranger who just spoke to me. A man, dressed in black, is hanging from my ceiling. How the fuck did I not notice him?

Simple. I was thinking of dismembered children. Sue me.

He doesn't move, not showing any signs that he's about to jump me. He isn't here to kill me, that much is obvious. He could have done so easily already. How did he even get in? The window is locked from the inside, and there are traps all around it, so definitely not that way. That means he must have come from downstairs. He walked through our house, and nobody noticed. I need to have a word with my colleagues. This is ridiculous, someone breaking into the headquarters of an assassin business.

"What do you want?" I snap, glaring up at him.

He's wearing a black jumpsuit with a wide hood that hides most of his face. Even so, I'm pretty sure I've never met him before. The way he moves, his voice, his smell. None of them rings a bell.

"You've stumbled across some interesting things, am I right?" he asks with a small laugh. It's not a question. He knows what I've been up to. A suspicion rises in me, but I keep my cards close to my chest for now.

"Everything in my life is interesting," I quip. "What do you know about it?"

He laughs. "Yes, a cat leading a group of ragtag criminals. Not quite what I expected when I found this card."

He flicks something and I catch it. My business card. I don't give them to just anybody. I hold it to my nose and sniff. Caitlin. The girl from the sweet shop.

"She's dead," he says matter of factly. "I found this on her body."

"Did you kill her?" I ask just as calmly.

"Maybe. Would you be upset about it?"

I shrug. "Depends. She may have been involved in something bad and if that's true, then go ahead. Kill her again, if you want to."

He smiles and moves a little. Immediately, I have my

knives ready to throw, but he's only stretching his arms. He must be sore from clinging to the ceiling beams for so long. Who knows how long he's been waiting in here for me.

"Want to come down so we can talk properly?" I suggest, eyeing him warily.

He nods, and with a graceful backflip, he lands next to me, not even swaying. Wow. That landing was worthy of a cat. Who the fuck is he?

"You know who I am, but who are you?" I ask.

"A friend. A partner in crime. An interested party. Pick one."

"I'd rather you tell me."

"We have the same enemy. Not sure what that makes us."

He flaunts over to my hammock and sits down on it, leaving me no choice but to remain standing. I don't have any other furniture in my attic, save a wooden chest that hides my messy assortment of clothes. I've never touched an iron in my life and I don't intend to, unless I'd need to use it as a weapon. Who cares about crinkles. The dead certainly don't.

"Was she involved?" I ask. "Caitlin?"

He throws back his hood, exposing a face that would make other people falter. Three large scars run from his right temple all the way down to his left jaw. Like he was clawed by a beast. Something big. If it wasn't for the scars, he could probably be called attractive. His eyes are bright green, not quite emerald but something lighter, like sun shining on fresh grass. A beard graces his cheeks, interrupted by the puckered lines of his scars.

His dark brown hair is bound back, but I can't see how long it is.

"She was. She had a sense for which children were shifters. She sent them on errands, telling them they could earn some extra pocket money. They never returned, obviously. I think you may have found parts of them at the laboratory."

I suppress a shudder. "How do you know so much?"

He doesn't reply to my question. Instead, he looks at me, and I have the feeling he's weighing me up. Judging whether I'm the right person for whatever he's planning.

I take it as an opportunity to take in more of him. His body is lithe and toned. A predator ready to fight. His shoulders are narrower than Lennox's, but he's a little taller. Why the heck am I comparing him to Lennox? It's not like there aren't any other men in this town to take as examples.

Finally, he stops his examination and meets my eyes. "I killed him. Kindler. And I also killed Caitlin. And quite a few other people, if you must know."

He confirms what I'd already suspected. He's the assassin whose work I admired.

"Who else?"

He chuckles. "The man whose house you broke into today. One of the people owning the flat near the market. Some others you didn't come across and won't now because, well, they're no longer there."

"Then why are you here?" I challenge him. "Looks like you've got it all under control. Killing one after the other until everyone involved in this is dead."

"If only it was that easy. I've come to the end of

what I can achieve on my own. I've realised this is much bigger than I first assumed. Whenever I kill one person, three more take their place. It's time to go after the people behind it all, not the henchmen."

He probably means the Fangs, but I'm not going to reveal that I know about them. So I just nod, studying him.

"So you want to pool resources and go after the head of the snake?"

"Aye. You seem to have come quite far in a very short time, so it seemed you'd be a good partner. It's taken me months to put it all together."

"Months? How long have they been giving poison to children?"

"About two months, but they started their experiments long before that. I first noticed something fishy was going on when two shifter kids disappeared from where I lived. I wasn't close to them or anything, but it intrigued me. Turns out they were two of the first who were used in those experiments."

A shiver runs over my back. The thought that anyone would harm children still gets to me. It squeezes through the tight assassin walls I've built around my emotions. Damn it. Now's not the time to start acting human.

"We should meet with that other man of yours, and your team."

"He's not my man," I snap, but the assassin just grins at me.

"It looked like a date to me. He even got you flowers."

"None of your business."

He shrugs. "I like the name, by the way. Meow. Very imaginative."

I snort. "Yeah, totally creative. But if you want me to introduce you to my team, I need to know more about you."

He crosses his arms behind his head and relaxes on my hammock. What an arrogant bastard. I'm not sure yet if I like him or not. His manner is frustrating, but it's also a bit like looking into a mirror.

"The name's Gryphon. I'm a freelancer like you, except that I work alone."

"You're not a shifter," I state, confident because he doesn't smell like one of us. Still, he doesn't seem quite human, not with the way he clung to my ceiling.

"I'm not," he says simply, but doesn't expand on what he actually is.

"What are you? I'm going to find out at some point or another, so better tell me now."

He grins lazily. "I'm human."

"No, you're not."

"I'm human, I'm telling you. Human with a bit of extra magic."

"Magic?" I snort. "Magic doesn't exist. Not like in the books. No wands and wizards and spells."

He sighs. "Do you always take things so literally? I'm human, as I said, but I also have some abilities that are non-human. And that's all I'm going to say about that. Just be reassured that I will be able to match you without problem. I'm not some weakling who gets exhausted after two miles of running."

"I never suggested that," I protest, but then shut up, realising that he baited me. Oh well. I'm going to learn all about him, whether he wants it or not. I have my cats, my secret weapon that not even Lennox knows about. Not sure I'm going to tell him. It's nice to have the upper hand in that aspect.

"You're not associated with the Pack or some other organisation?" I ask just to make sure.

He laughs. "If I was, you wouldn't be alive. No, I'm a freelancer. I pick my own contracts, just like you. I stay out of the Pack's way as much as I can. I'm not stupid, I know how powerful they are. But now, it seems we have no choice but to act against them."

We. He's already thinking of us as a team. That was quick, but he's probably planned this for a while.

"When did you find out that I was investigating the case?" I ask, continuing the investigation.

"I was waiting near the sweet shop to have a long chat with Caitlin, but then you showed up, simply walking in there, ignoring the children. I was curious, so I followed you. Good job finding the clues in Kindler's house, but I already removed the lockbox the key was for."

"What was in it?"

"Contracts confirming that he was working for the Healers."

"Healers?"

"Ah, you don't know that bit yet. That's what they call themselves, the people who came up with the idea of poisoning children. I think they see it as healing the world from shifters. They see us as a disease that needs to be eliminated."

"They could have come up with a better name," I mutter. "Something like Slaughterers or Abominations."

Gryphon chuckles. "I agree, but it's a bit too late to suggest they change it. Anyway, unless you have more questions, I have places to be. Let's meet tomorrow with your team and your boyfriend."

I lift one of my daggers to throw at him, but he's already jumped out of the hammock and throws himself through the trap door, ignoring the ladder going down. Idiot.

"Tomorrow at ten!" he shouts, and all I can do is sigh.

What a strange, strange man. I seem to attract them recently. Lennox is strange too, in his own wolfy way. And now a not-quite-human assassin. But I can't let them distract me. Too much is at stake. If we don't stop those Healers now, there may not be many shifters left in the future.

After a nap and a shower, I head down into the kitchen. It's empty, and I'm kind of relieved. I don't want to deal with people just yet. Too much socialising in the past couple of days. I miss my silent nights of wandering across the roofs of the town, alone.

I grab a sandwich and head out to the backyard. Just like I expected, three cats are waiting there. Pan, the dark female ginger who looks so fluffy that I have to stop myself from running my hands through her fur; Mila the tabby and one I haven't met before. A small but feral looking Bengal cat with round brown splotches on his back and delicate stripes around his neck. His tail is very straight; it kind of looks like he's got a stick pointing out of his arse. Not that I'll tell him that. I'm not suicidal.

"Have you been fed yet?" I ask and feel three notions of assent. Good. My team seem to have got used to the idea of having to look after a horde of hungry cats. Benjamin seems to really enjoy it.

I sit down on one of the stone plant pots that we've never bothered to actually fill with something green.

"Did you see the man who just left the house? All in black, walks like a predator?"

Mila nods.

"He's on our side, but I want you to keep an eye on him. Find out what he is. Where he lives. What he does. I want to know everything about him."

She bows her head. Pan meows loudly.

"Want me to shift?"

She stares at me with lime green eyes and I sigh. I thought I could go back to my hammock and read a book. Work's never done.

I eat the last bits of my sandwich and shift. I take a moment to stretch my tired limbs, extending my claws. I love the way that feels. It's an itch I can never scratch as a human.

I look down at the three cats which now seem even smaller. None of them seem even slightly scared of me though. It's kind of disappointing.

"The old human you wanted us to follow. The one with the weird ears."

"Ears?"

Pan sighs in exasperation. "Black thing on his hat. Looks like a square ear."

The top hat that my mysterious benefactor likes to wear. Of course, cats wouldn't have a concept of what a hat is for.

"What did he do?" I ask.

"He came close to here, but he didn't enter the house. I think he was waiting for something or someone. It was strange. He behaved like one of us."

I laugh, a roar escaping my throat.

"When was that?"

"Not long. I licked my paws twice since," the third cat says with a yawn. He's not introduced himself yet, so I politely ask him for his name.

"James," he replies, his accent a little posh. Bengal cats are expensive. If he's had an owner before he became a stray, I bet he had a good upbringing.

"Do you know where he is now?"

"Ryker is keeping an eye on him. I've smelled him recently so they must be nearby. Shall I find out?" Pan asks and I nod.

"If he's close, I want to speak to him."

Pan runs off, jumping up the stone wall in one elegant leap. The other two cats lie down as if they assume that there's no more to discuss. Suits me well. I stretch again, then search for a sunny spot to take a nap myself. The evening sun is disappearing quickly, but the stone ground is still warm enough to be comfy. I close my eyes and relax. Being a cat is so much better than walking around as a stressed human.

Before I can properly fall asleep, a warm nose bumps against me. I blink open one eye and stare at Pan. Her fluffy fur is even prettier from up close, shiny and soft. I wish mine was like that. I mean, my fur is silky black, but not very smooth. Not that anyone gets to pet me. Lily tried it once, and I almost bit off her hand. I'm a cat. I'm proud.

"They're two streets away," Pan informs me. "Ryker is waiting there for you. The man is still standing at a corner, not moving. Ryker finds him very strange, but he wants you to make your own picture."

I sigh and get up, shaking my entire body, relaxing my muscles. Time to become human again. It sucks.

CHAPTER EIGHTEEN

"Good evening."

Mystery man whirls around, clearly surprised by my presence. I didn't even try to be quiet. He must have been deep in thought.

"What are you doing here?" he asks, suspicion glinting in his eyes.

I shrug. "Taking an evening walk. Beautiful light, isn't it."

He frowns, making his facial scars move. "There are a lot of cats around here," he states, but I don't respond. "If I didn't know any better, I'd say that one has been following me. But that's impossible, right?"

"Right," I say without conviction. "That would be very strange."

The man chuckles. "I knew you were resourceful, but this takes it to an entirely new level. Maybe I can trust you with this after all."

"With what?"

"Let's take this somewhere else. The streets have ears, and not all of them are feline."

By the time we get back to the house, Lily is in the kitchen, rummaging around.

I sneak in and ask her to make some tea for two.

"Do we have a visitor?" she asks and I nod.

"I'll tell you later. We'll be in the office."

She gives me a curious look, but I don't have any time to waste. Mystery Man is already in my office, and I suspect he's going through my things. It's what I would do, and I have a feeling that he's rather similar to me.

When I enter the room, he's sitting on my large office chair. I swallow a comment and take a seat on the chair usually reserved for visitors. Yes, I guess the house used to be his and therefore this leather chair as well, but it still stings.

"My colleague is making us some tea," I tell him and he smiles.

"Your colleague? Not your employee?"

"I don't believe in hierarchies. We each focus on what we do best. I occasionally take the lead, and I look after the business side of things, but besides that, we're all colleagues."

He rubs his chin. "Interesting. I've found you intriguing ever since we first met. I almost wish we had time to get to know each other, but as always, time is of the essence. I know I told you to stay away from the Kindler case, but a new development has arisen."

Lily knocks on the door, and I quickly get up and take the two mugs of tea she's prepared, before closing the door behind me. I trust her not to listen in, but only because she knows that I'll tell her everything later on.

Mystery man gives the tea a suspicious look.

"No poison," I reassure him.

He chuckles. "I wasn't worried about that. I just doubt the quality of the tea. It's not the sort of tea I usually drink."

I don't deign him with a reply. It's good tea. Well, the standard stuff you can buy in the shop. It does the job. It's certainly better than the murky water I was served at the cafe with Lennox.

He puts the mug on my desk - using a stack of paper as a coaster - and looks at me with an intense expression.

"My granddaughter has fallen ill," he says without preamble. "I'm worried it might be the poison. She didn't go to the sweet shop because I told her not to, but she seems to have eaten some sweets that a friend offered her at school. Maybe it's unrelated, but the doctor can't make sense of the symptoms. They don't fit any disease he knows of, and neither do they sound like the standard poisons I'm aware of."

I sit up straight. So far, we've not known what the poison in the sweets actually does to children. But if his granddaughter is suffering from its effect... things could go bad very quickly.

"Do you know of any other children who've fallen sick?"

He shakes his head. "I don't mingle with children. She's the only one because she's family."

He says it with a certain distaste. Not exactly how I imagine a grandfather, but well, he's Mystery Man. He's allowed to be weird.

"Give me one moment." I get up and walk to one of the windows. Outside on the window sill is Pumpkin, Ryker's son, the kitten who started it all. He loves that spot for some reason, even though it must be a pain to reach since we're on the second floor.

"Pumpkin, I need you to find out if a lot of children are ill at the moment. They'd be at home, in bed, rather than be playing outside or going to school. This is important, I need to know as soon as possible."

He jumps off before I can say anything else, disappearing into the night.

"Good boy," I whisper, then immediately feeling a little silly about it. I'm beginning to sound like a crazy cat lady whose house is full of felines and who can't focus on anything but her pets. That's not me. Not at all.

"I'll check out some of the schools tomorrow," I say, returning to my seat. "How ill is your granddaughter?"

"She's vomiting a lot. She says she has the urge to shift but she can't. It's driving her crazy. She started scratching her arms earlier today, saying that she could feel her fur underneath her skin and that it wanted to come out. That's when I decided that something needed to be done."

"That means we're now no longer just looking to close them down, but also to find a cure," I summarise with a sigh. "Any idea where to start?"

"I know some of the people involved," he admits. "People you don't want to mess with. Usually, I'd tell you to stay far away from them, but it's no longer about us. It's about shifter children like my granddaughter. I'll write down the addresses of the ringleaders, at least the ones I know. I can't be seen to get involved, there's too much at stake. A lot of lives depend on me staying in the shadows."

He's being very mysterious, but I don't call him out on it. I have other priorities.

"I'll have a chat with them," I say, already debating what tools to take with me. This is going to get ugly. "If there's a cure, I will find out. Trust me. I know how to make people talk."

"They'll be well-protected and armed," he warns. "Tread carefully. If one of them warns the others, you'll have no chance of getting to them."

"How many are there?"

"Three that I have addresses for. Probably more but maybe you can get their names during your interrogation."

I give him a grin. "You're in luck. I know two others who are perfect for the job. How do I contact you?"

He hands me a black business card. On one side, it has an embossed silver ouroboros, a snake eating its own tail, and on the other side is a phone number. No name, no address.

"You take your privacy very serious, don't you," I quip.

He doesn't reply, and I didn't expect him to. Not everyone can have fancy Meow business cards like me.

"I'll contact you if I find out anything else," he says and gets up from my chair. "Stay safe."

He leaves without another word, his tea untouched. I almost take that as an insult. My tea is good. I could have given him poison, but I didn't. I'm a good person. With good tea.

I REALLY WANT TO SLEEP, BUT THINKING OF A LITTLE GIRL in pain makes me decide otherwise. I write two quick notes and ask some cats to bring them to Lennox and Gryphon. I doubt either of them expected to hear from me again so soon, but this is an emergency. The cats look at me in annoyance but accept their errands when I promise them treats.

Sadly, this means that the two men might figure out that I'm employing cats. Hopefully, they'll assume it's just to use them as carrier cats rather than spies. I'd hate to give up that secret. Still, saving children's lives is more important. If they find out that I have two dozen cats at my disposal, then so be it.

I fill in the others while we wait for the men to show up.

"I'm glad you progressed with the case," Lily says once I'm done. "Winston's brother was an absolute bore. I doubt he knows anything about what his brother did or why he was killed. I wish I could get the time back I spent with him."

She purses her lips in distaste. "You said he was hot."

I smile innocently. "Did I? You must have misheard." I turn to the other two. "Beth, I want you to continue experimenting with the poison. Maybe you can figure out how it works, what it does and how to undo its effects. If you need more of the substance, I'm sure Benjamin can get you some more from the flat near the market."

Both of them nod. The mood has been sombre ever since I told them that someone had experimented on kids.

"Benjamin, I need you to find out how many children have been affected. You're the youngest of us, so you'll blend in best. Go to schools, nurseries, whatever. I've told the cats to do the same thing, but they can't ask questions. You can. Mystery man's granddaughter might not be the only one affected, and who knows if she was the first. Others could have already died without us knowing."

"On it, boss," Benjamin says, his voice serious. "I still have contacts who're not part of the Pack, I'll see if they've heard anything about children going missing."

"What do you want me to do?" Lily asks. "Want me to come with you?"

I shake my head. "No, I want you to work with Beth on the poison. That's our priority right now. As much as I want to kill everyone involved, we need to find a cure to help the children who ate those blasted sweets."

"We've made some progress already," Beth tells me proudly. "We started with testing for all the usual poisons, and it didn't match any of them. But then I had the idea-"

"It was my idea," Lily interrupts.

Beth shrugs. "Semantics. *We* had the idea to add some luminol."

"What's that?" Benjamin asks. He's never spent much time in the lab.

"It's a chemical that glows blue when it's mixed with oxidants," I explain. "Including the iron contained in blood. You can spray it on walls to see if you've created a pretty splatter pattern. It's great fun."

Lily clears her throat. "Anyway... there's definitely dried blood in the powder. Not a whole lot but enough to show up when mixed with luminol. And yes, we checked whether it could be other oxidants, but all tests were negative. It's blood."

"Is there a way to tell if it's human or shifter blood?" I ask.

Lily grins. "I was hoping you'd ask that. We think that we might be able to find out if we had some blood to compare it with. Yours, namely. Then one of us can donate some human blood, and maybe we can get one of the cats to give us some of theirs. To have a non-humanoid comparison."

Benjamin jumps off the sofa and runs out of the room. "I'll see if there's one outside."

"He's become obsessed," Lily mutters. "He's been spoiling them, giving them far more food than you agreed to."

I shrug. "I don't mind. They're worth their weight in catnip."

A deep meow makes me turn towards the door, and I regret my words. Ryker is one big moggy. He'll weigh as much as a fortune in cat food.

I get up and kneel on the floor, getting closer to

Ryker's eye level. I don't want him to feel like we're all towering high above him.

"Good evening," I say, and he purrs in return. Once again, I'm tempted to run a hand through his fur. He's absolutely beautiful with his silver-black coat and his bright yellow eyes. I bet he has a swarm of lady cats following him wherever he goes.

"We need some blood from a cat for a test. It's important, I wouldn't ask otherwise. Would you or one of your friends be willing to have some blood taken? We only need a small amount."

He looks into my eyes, and I feel like he's judging me. Deciding whether it's worth doing this for me or not. After at least a minute of staring, he meows.

I sigh. "What are your demands?"

CHAPTER NINETEEN

I rub my arm where Beth poked me with a cannula. She's not going to pursue a career in nursing any time soon. I would have bruises if I wasn't a shifter with fast healing abilities. Poor Ryker ran away as soon as she was done, hissing like crazy.

Gryphon, Lennox and I have split up, each moving towards one of the three addresses Mystery Man gave me. I check my watch. Another two minutes until I can strike. We're going to do it simultaneously so that there's absolutely no chance of them contacting each other. This needs to be quick and efficient. Interrogate them, kill them, then find additional clues about their plans. Dare I hope that one of them keeps a detailed diary with all his evil plans written down? That would make my day. No more searching for the needle in a murderous haystack. Just simple, straightforward answers.

Could life be boring for once? Just this time?

One more minute. I move closer to the edge of the

roof, all my senses on full alert. There are two people in the house beneath me; one sleeping, one moving around on the ground floor. I don't know which of them is the important one, or if both of them are worth interrogating, so I'm going to have to knock one out without alerting the second. Usually, not all that difficult, but this entire case has been so full of twists and turns that by now I always expect the worse.

There's a small balcony on the floor below, my way into the house. I'm not stupid enough to walk through the front door. Now that I know it wasn't the Healers themselves who killed Winston Kindler, they must be on high alert, knowing that someone is out there who knows what's going on. On the one hand, I want to blame Gryphon for acting rashly, especially with killing Caitlin, but he was trying to stop more people from getting poisoned. Who could have known about the clause in Mr Kinder's will that said that all his remaining sweets were to be given to children for free? We don't know yet if all those sweets were poisoned, but let's expect the worst.

Midnight. Time to strike. I drop down onto the balcony, landing on all fours without making a sound. I get to work on the balcony doors, unlocking them within seconds. Someone didn't think of people entering this way. How pathetic.

I walk into the quiet house, knives at the ready in case someone surprises me. But that's unlikely. I've still got my senses focused on the two people, one below me, one straight ahead. A faint snoring is coming from nearby. That will make things even easier. I slowly prowl along the corridor towards the bedroom. I don't tiptoe like they do on television. That just makes you unsteady and more likely to trip.

The door to the bedroom is closed, but I'm well versed in opening a wooden door without it creaking. This one is old, but it's no match for me. I push it with just enough pressure to move it, but not make a sound. It's something I learned as a toddler. There's a certain seventh sense to it, a feeling that tells you when to stop and when to put your hands lower or higher to avoid a creak. It's hard to explain.

All the while, the snoring continues along with regular deep breaths. The man is fast asleep. From my pocket, I pull a tiny vial and empty it onto a cotton handkerchief. I stop breathing, not wanting to feel the effects of the drug myself. I crouch low and move towards the bed, staying low enough that even if the man suddenly opens his eyes, I won't be in his line of sight. As soon as I reach him, I hold the handkerchief above his face. Only after he's taken a few more breaths do I press it hard on his nose and mouth. By now, he's already so deep asleep that he won't be able to react. I take his wrist and measure his pulse while waiting for him to become unconscious enough for me to move him. When his heartbeat has slowed down enough, I remove the handkerchief and place it in a sealed bag before stuffing it into my pocket.

The other person is moving around on the ground floor, and there's no time to waste. I stuff a cloth into the man's mouth and bind his hands and legs. I doubt he'll wake up in the next hour or so, but better safe than sorry.

Time for the second human to be subdued. This one will be a little harder because he's awake. I leave the bedroom, quietly closing the door again to hide my tracks.

Heading towards the staircase, I keep my focus on the other person. Now that I'm getting closer, I sniff the air. It's a woman. Interesting. So far, everyone involved in this has been male, except Caitlin but she was just a small fish in a pond full of sharks.

She is moving around from room to room. What the hell is she doing? She's either an insomniac who's trying to get some exercise by pacing back and forth, or she's looking for something. Maybe she's not connected to the man I just drugged? Perhaps she's a thief - but no, for that, she's very loud and careless. Even a novice would know better than to make such a racket.

With so many unknowns, I decide to take a page out of Gryphon's book. Remembering how he surprised me, I grin and launch myself into the air. The chandelier on the ceiling above the stairwell swings violently when I grab hold of it, but it carries my weight. Good. I wasn't entirely sure it would be strong enough. Reckless but fun.

I wait until the chandelier has stopped moving, then clear my throat, making my voice as deep as possible.

"Help!" I rasp. Of course, I have no idea what the man in the bed sounds like, but I've made it muffled enough that it should be believable. People in danger rarely sound like they usually do.

Immediately, the sounds below stop. One breath. Two. She's trying to figure out what to do. Then she starts running towards the staircase. I can't help but smile when she comes into view. She's a big woman, twice as wide as me but a tiny bit shorter. She's wearing a pink suit that reminds me of a sausage skin and hair that would make an excellent bird's nest. Not what I expected.

She runs up the stairs, huffing and puffing. This is going to be an easy one.

"Philip?" she calls out when she reaches the top step.

I don't let her get any further. I drop down right behind her and have a knife pressed against her throat before she can even turn.

"Don't make a sound," I hiss.

She freezes.

"Good. Now walk with me towards that wall. Very nice. Stretch up your arms and put your palms against the wall."

With one practised hand, I tie her wrists together while keeping the knife so close to her skin that it's a constant reminder of what might happen if she struggles.

"Let's go and have a chat," I whisper menacingly and push her into the room closest to us. It's an office with two large desks and matching high-back chairs. Every wall is lined with bookshelves, all of them filled with folders, notebooks and cardboard boxes.

"Sit."

I shove the woman towards an expensive leather chair, and she obediently sits down, breathing hard. The smell of sweat fills my nostrils, and I relax my cat senses a little to return to my human sense of smell.

"What do you want?" she asks with a high-pitched, shaky voice.

I ignore her and bind her legs to the chair, then wrap another rope around her ample waist. I attach her wrists to the arms of the chair, nice and exposed for my future plans. By the time I've got her secured, she's become a little less scared and is glaring at me.

"You have no idea who you're dealing with, girl. You better let me go, and I might stay quiet about what you've just done."

I laugh. Did she just call me 'girl'? I'm going to show her that I'm nothing remotely as innocent as that. I scratch my nose with one of my knives, and she immediately shuts up. Nice to know she's quick in understanding a well-placed hint.

"I'm asking the questions," I state. "And we can do this the quick and easy, or the painful and drawn-out way. You're going to tell me everything eventually. It's your decision on how much it's going to hurt."

She blanches a little but stays quiet.

"Oh, and I'm going to interrogate the other guy too," I say as an afterthought. "If your statements don't match, I'm going to have to be more... persuasive." I smile at her.

Her eyelids flicker and a tear runs down her cheek. Pathetic.

"Please don't hurt me," she whimpers. "I don't know anything."

I don't believe her for a second. Besides, her heartbeat tells me all I need to know.

I drag another chair over and sit down so close to her that our knees are touching. Invading her personal space results in her leaning back, but there's nowhere for her to move.

"Let's start with the easy questions," I purr. "What's your name?"

"Elizabeth," she says far too quickly.

"You're lying." I take my biggest knife and casually lay it across my thighs. "Tell me your name."

"Constance Green."

This time, her heartbeat doesn't increase. Good. Seems like we're getting somewhere.

"Why are you here, Constance?"

"This is my home."

Truth.

"And what were you doing down there? It sounded like you were rather busy."

She hesitates for a moment. "I was looking for my glasses. I keep losing them."

I can't help it, I have to laugh. "A world of excuses and you came up with that one? Come on, Constance, you're starting to make this difficult for yourself."

"They're going to kill me if I tell you anything," she whispers. "You don't know how dangerous they are."

I look at her unimpressed. "Trust me, I do. And I couldn't care less. Tell me what you were doing."

She purses her lips, her scared expression making way for determination. "I was looking for my glasses."

Seriously? I sigh and get up, pulling a needle from my collar. I hold it up in front of her so she can see.

"Do you know what they used to do to witches? They pricked them with needles to see if they had a devil's mark beneath their skin. It may not sound very frightening, but this needle is dipped in poison. Every prick will feel like a cut with a knife. Without the blood. Handy, isn't it?"

Without warning, I jab the needle into her cheek. She screams, flinging her head from side to side, but there's no escaping the pain. I know how much it hurts. They didn't just do this to witches. The Pack uses the same technique to force children to shift.

I give her half a minute to recover, then I repeat my question for the third time.

"What were you doing? What are you hiding?"

She glares at me. "I'm not going to tell you."

Her cheek has turned red and is starting to swell. The effect won't last; she'll be good as new in an hour or so.

"Do you know what happens if don't remove the needle immediately after the prick?" I ask her sweetly. "Do you want to find out?"

She shakes her head, but I ignore her. This time, I pierce her thigh. It doesn't have to be deep, just enough to break the skin and release the poison. Constance screams in agony, fighting against her bonds. She's stronger than I expected, but I'm confident her bonds will hold. Ropework is one of my lesser known talents.

"This time I took it out," I tell her while waiting for her to stop trembling. "But next time, I might leave it in for a bit. Maybe I could leave you here while I talk to the other guy. How does that sound?"

She shoots me a hateful glare. "Go to hell, bitch."

First girl, then bitch. That woman really doesn't have any manners. I shrug and take out a second needle. The first one will have very little poison on it by now, but it's still enough to be effective one more time. I poke them both into her knees. Most people don't know this, but knees are one of the places where a lot of nerves lie unprotected, waiting to be stimulated.

"Last chance," I whisper into her ear. "Next time, they're staying."

She opens her mouth and spits at me. A splotch of saliva hits my collar bone. Alright, she doesn't want to be cooperative. I can stop playing nice. This time, I opt for the tips of her fingers. It's an amazingly effective spot. A papercut can make a grown man cry, and my poisoned needles hurt a lot more than a papercut.

She howls in pain, struggling so hard that she's making the chair sway from side to side. I get up and look down at her in satisfaction. With both her wrists tied to the chair's arms, she has no way of removing the needles.

"I'll leave you to it," I say lightly and move to leave the room. "Remember, I gave you the chance to do this the painless way. You were too stupid to take it."

She flings a string of insults at me, but I simply close the door behind me and ignore her. She's going to be a lot more pliable when I return.

CHAPTER TWENTY

Turns out the man is more cooperative than the woman. After a bit of tying up, needle pricking and a lot of threats, his tongue loosens immensely.

"Those abominations need to be exterminated."

I only listen with one ear, unwilling to give him the satisfaction of having an audience for his craziness.

"One day, if we don't do anything now, they'll take over. They'll subjugate us humans and make us work for them."

"Like they now work for you as part of the Pack?" I can't help but interject. He just glares at me, but it's clear that he knows I'm right. The Pack is built on enslaving shifters, turning them into thugs and killers to earn money for their owners.

"They're too violent to be left running free. They'd kill us all."

I sigh. "We kill because humans train us to. It's kill or be killed. Which option would you choose?"

"We?" he cries. "You're one of them?"

For a second, I let my panther take over, knowing that my eyes will change colour. He gasps and tries to move away from me, but he's tied to the bed, unable to do anything more than wriggle.

"Let's talk about the poison," I say, speeding up the conversation a little. "What does it do exactly?"

He frowns at me. "You don't know."

"It doesn't matter what I know or don't," I snap. "Answer my question."

To emphasise my words, I pull another needle from my hidden stash sewn into my collar. His eyes widen and his heart rate increases. Good. He's learned his lesson.

"It's supposed to suppress the shift," he whispers. "Make them human."

"Supposed to?"

"We didn't get it to work as intended in time. We had a deadline and we didn't meet it, so we gave out the half-finished version instead."

"Who gave you that deadline?"

"If I tell you that, I'm dead."

I grin. "If you don't, you're dead too. You basically have to decide how quickly you want to die. Today or at some unknown day in the future?"

His expression turns more and more defeated. "Some very powerful people. That's all I can tell you. I never even talked to them myself. I'm not one of the leaders, I just head up the lab. You need to ask Constance about that."

Oh, so the woman is higher up in the hierarchy than him? Good to know.

"The current poison, the unfinished version, what does it do?" I ask, dreading the answer.

"Kill them, I think. All the test subjects died. We managed to keep them alive for longer, but in the end, none of them survived. There weren't enough to come to a final conclusion, but the probability that the current substance is still lethal is high. Now that it's been given to hundreds of shifters, there's a chance that some of them may survive, but nobody knows for sure. It will be interesting to see."

I'm stunned. He's talking about children dying without even realising it. For him, it's science, medical experiments, something he believes in. I'm going to enjoy killing him.

"Is there an antidote?" I ask sharply.

He smiles, surprising me. "I'm not going to tell you that. You're not going to destroy all of our work. In the end, it doesn't matter if they can't shift or if they die. The result is the same. No more shifters. Even with the unfinished product, we've still succeeded."

"Yes, you're going to tell me. One way or another."

He clamps his jaws and glares at me, making it clear that he has no intention of doing so.

I rummage in my pockets until I find a small yellow vial.

"You're a scientist, so I assume you know what Bishop's Mantle is?"

He blanches visibly but doesn't reply.

"It's a plant that produces a very intense nerve poison," I continue. "It starts acting slow, paralysing your extremities, then slowly moving through your body, shutting down your organs one by one. All while giving you terrible pain. The heart and lungs are the last organs to still work. You'll be conscious the entire time, realising that you're dying, but are unable to move, unable to do anything about it. You won't even be able to scream. I'm told the pain is unimaginable by the time your heart is affected. It can take hours to die, even up to a day. Do you really want this? Is it worth it?"

His heartbeat is racing, and sweat is pearling on his forehead. I can smell his fear even with my human senses.

When he still doesn't respond, I flick open the vial and sit down on the bed beside him.

"Last chance," I whisper, holding the little flask close to his mouth.

His eyes have turned white with panic. He's about to break. Just a tiny bit closer… the vial touches his bottom lip and he cries out.

"There is!"

I sit back a little but keep the poison in his line of sight.

"Tell me more," I encourage him, smiling despite his hateful glare.

"It only works within the first two days of the shifter poison being administered, after that, it has no effect," he says hastily, his eyes never leaving the vial. "That's why it was of no use to us. We needed the shifters to be further into the transformation, but they always died before they could get to the stage where they would no longer be able to shift. There's a stockpile near the lab, unless someone's thrown it away. As I said, we didn't have a use for it, we just produced one batch of it just in case we'd need it later on."

"One batch? How many doses?"

"A hundred at most. If it's still there."

We can save one hundred children. If there are that many left. Two days. How long has it been since Caitlin gave all those sweets away for free? Was that even in Mr Kindler's will or did she make that up since she was working for the Healers herself?

The flicker of hope I'd just felt dwindles down. Unless some of the shifter children waited with eating the sweets, or unless not all of the sweets were laced with poison, it's too late for all of them.

This is going to be a big problem. For each and every child, we need to know whether they're a shifter and how long ago they ate the sweets. Then decide whether it's worth giving them the antidote or not. How many children are there in this town? I don't even want to begin to guess. And what if he's lying? What if the antidote works no matter how long it's been? Are we going to let children die by believing him?

What a mess.

"Where's the cure being stored?"

He tells me the address, and I commit it to memory. Then I open the vial again and make him drink the Bishop's Mantle. He screams and writhes and begs, but I don't feel remotely tempted to have pity with him. He deserves to die in agony.

I decide that it's more important to distribute the antidote rather than interrogate Constance. That can wait till later, when time is less of the essence. I run across town using the fastest route I know, using mostly roofs and hidden alleyways.

By the time I get to the warehouse, I'm drenched in sweat. Even for me, that run was exhausting. I dispatch the two guards effortlessly, not making much of a fuss. I don't care about having their bodies lie in plain sight. I'll be long gone by the time anyone notices them, and right now, I don't have the time to erase my traces.

The warehouse is jam packed with metal containers, all of them looking the same. Fuck. How am I supposed to find anything in here? The only way…

I shift, hoping that my theory will work. I still have the scent of the man in my nose, the man who said he's handled the antidote before. I breathe in deep, concentrating on my sense of smell. Please let it work. Please.

I pace along the main corridor between the containers, sniffing from left to right and back again. I'm almost at the end when I can finally smell him. Yes, it's the same scent. I jump, following the trail with big leaps until I reach a battered looking container. Bingo.

Instead of trying to claw it open, I shift back to human, groaning at the pain. Shifting twice within such a short period can be painful, especially if I have to hurry. Still, it can't be helped.

Wincing, I pick the padlock and open the container door. Inside are dozens of crates stacked into wobbly looking towers. Have these people never heard of labels?! This is getting ridiculous, and my sense of smell won't help me in here. I bet the human has touched most of the things in this container.

I start pulling crates off their stacks and opening them, randomly pulling out the items inside. Nothing interesting. One box has about a thousand metal spoons in it. If I had the time, I'd wonder what the hell they're planning to do with those, but I need to find what I'm really looking for. Finally, after at least ten minutes of frantic searching, I find a small cardboard box within one of the crates, containing ten bottles filled with tiny blue pills.

I open one of the bottles and give it a sniff. It smells similar to the poison, but it's not quite the same. One of the other bottles even has a scribbled label.

A.dote.

This must be it. The cure.

I just hope there are children left to heal.

CHAPTER TWENTY-ONE

It doesn't take me long to find two cats that belong to Ryker's group. I tie a blue ribbon around both their necks; the sign I agreed with Lennox and Gryphon that we need to reassemble as soon as possible. They run off, and I trust they will find the two assassins soon. Other cats have been shadowing them ever since we left the Meow headquarters, so it shouldn't be too hard.

I run home as fast as I can, carefully clutching the pill bottles. Somehow, I'm scared to even put them into my pockets. I want to keep an eye on them at all times. They're our last hope to save the sick shifter children.

Ryker is waiting for me outside my home. He meows as soon as he sees me and stands up on his hind feet, obviously seeking my attention.

"I don't have time," I tell him in frustration. "Is it urgent?"

He nods, and I can feel how he's trying to tell me mentally that it's important for him to talk to me.

I sigh. "Give me two minutes to hand these to Lily and then I'll come meet you in the backyard."

He gives me one more stern look, then runs off. Urgh. I'm going to have to shift again. This time, it's going to be really fucking painful.

Lily is in the lab with Beth. Both of them look at me expectantly as soon as I enter.

"I have the antidote," I say, surprised by how exhausted my voice sounds. "Take it and see if you can analyse one of the pills. We need to know if there's a way to replicate them. These are all we have, and who knows how many shifter children are out there."

I don't tell them yet that it might only work on very few of the children.

They get to work without another word, while I go upstairs to call Mystery Man. I could probably ask one of the cats to carry a message to him, but this will be quicker.

He answers on the first ring.

"I've got the cure," I say without wasting time on greetings. "You can collect it here for your granddaughter."

Silence meets my words.

Then, the sound of him clearing his throat.

"It's too late for that. She passed away twenty minutes ago."

I drop the phone. Fuck. We were too late. A shifter child, murdered, dead because of some humans who didn't even know the girl. They think we're the monsters, but, in fact, they are.

I want to cry, shout, hurt someone, but all I do is hang up the phone and walk outside. There's nothing I can do or say to make it better.

Ryker is waiting for me. I don't say anything, just shift, ignoring the pain. It feels almost good to have this physical pain to focus on rather than the emotional agony that's tearing at my heart.

"What's wrong?" Ryker asks in his melodic voice. He gently puts one paw on my much bigger one, and I look at him surprise. I didn't expect such a tender gesture from him. For a cat, he seems very emotionally intelligent.

I almost don't tell him, but then the words tumble from my mouth before I can stop them. "One of the children died. The granddaughter of the man who gave me this house. I've got a cure now, but we're too late. Most of the children will die. Maybe all of them. We've failed, Ryker. There's nothing we can do but sit and watch them perish."

He hisses, and suddenly, his claws are piercing the top of my claw. I growl at him, confused why he'd suddenly turn hostile.

"You're not a dog who simply lies down and covers his eyes when life doesn't do what he wants," Ryker snarls. "You're a cat. We don't give up. We keep persevering, even if it all looks hopeless. Yes, one child has died, and it's tragic, but there are many more out there who we might be able to help."

"We?" I ask, hating how pathetic and emotional I sound. I've never felt this weak in all my life.

"We. Together. You've got your humans and shifters, but us cats can help. We've found a way to find out which children have been poisoned."

I perk up a little. That would give us a massive advantage. We could target them straight away, giving them the antidote without having to ask every single child whether they've had sweets and whether they feel any ill effects.

"How?"

"They smell different," Ryker says matter-of-fact, as if I should have known that. Well, I probably should, but I've not actually met any poisoned child yet. "Your human thief has been helping us in discovering which smell means that they've eaten the treats."

"Benjamin?" I ask in confusion. "But he doesn't even understand you. He's not a shifter. He's just, well, human."

"He listens, he observes, and his body language is very expressive. He's built a bond with several of my family members, and somehow, they understand each other."

I mull over the new information. This could help immensely.

"I've been told that the cure I found will only save children who've eaten the poisoned sweets within the last two days. Do you think there's a way to smell who's ill and past that point?"

Ryker crocks his head. "Maybe. I'll check with

Storm, she's been leading on this. If there's a way, we'll find it. I'll be back as soon as I know more."

He pats my paw one more time and looks at me knowingly, then jumps up the wall surrounding the backyard and down on the other side.

I sigh and shift back, welcoming the pain.

Gryphon and Lennox arrive almost at the same time, both of them panting hard. They must have run the entire way, just like I did earlier. I give them a glass of water each and show them to the living room, where the other Meow members have assembled. Benjamin returned ten minutes ago, accompanied by a small white cat called Nyx. She lies at his feet, showing no intention of leaving. I ignore her. We have bigger fish to fry.

"Let's make this quick, we don't have much time," I announce, before giving them a quick summary of what's been happening.

"He lied," Gryphon says as soon as I've finished. "Or he didn't know any better. My mark, a guy pretty high up in the Healer hierarchy, said that the antidote is very effective. When I prodded him a little, he admitted that we could save every single child that they poisoned."

"He told you that?" Lily asks in surprise.

Gryphon grimaces. "It took a lot of persuading. He was almost dead by the time he finally divulged that last secret. I got a lot out of him though. Nothing that can't wait though." He looks at me and smiles. "You can stop looking so grim. We can save them. All of them."

"Some may already be dead, like Mystery Man's granddaughter," I say gloomily.

"Mystery Man?"

Ah. I haven't told him about my strange benefactor yet.

"Doesn't matter. If your guy didn't lie, then that means we can let the cats guide us to every single child who ate the sweets and give them an antidote. Until the pills run out, that is."

"Can the cats distinguish between shifters and humans?" Lennox asks.

I nod. "Easily. They always know immediately that I'm one of them. Kind of, anyway. And they've been keeping their distance from you because of that very same reason."

Lennox huffs. "I'm not a dog. Wolves and cats aren't all that different from each other."

"They beg to differ," I reply dryly. "Is there anything important that you found at your mark's house?"

He shakes his head. "Five easy kills. Didn't know much. They were just workers helping the Healers with their operation. I found some interesting documents though, but your messenger arrived before I could have a proper look. I've brought them with me to look at later."

"Were any of the people you guys killed part of the pack?" Beth asks.

"None of mine, at least I didn't recognise them," I

reply. "Although one of mine is still alive. Do you mind having a word with her? She was a little hesitant when I tried to get some answers, so I left her with some poisoned needles in her fingertips. She's going to be ready to talk by now."

Beth grins like I just gave her the best birthday present ever. "It will be my pleasure. I'll make her sing like a nightingale."

I nod. "Don't listen to her when she tries to pretend that she's low down in the pecking order. She's higher up than the man I interrogated and he headed up the lab. She must be important."

Bethany rubs her hands. "Even better. Do you want her alive after that?"

I shrug. "Not if she's given you all the information we need. Who else is involved? Have we cut off all the heads of the snake? Are the Fangs behind all of it? Who in the Pack sold the children for experimentation? That's just the short list of questions."

Beth sighs. "Alright, seems like I'll be busy for a while. I better go now. Good luck with the antidotes."

Once she's gone, Gryphon clears his throat. "I can answer one of those. The Fangs are definitely involved. I found some of their coins in my mark's house."

It only confirms what we all suspected already, but it makes the whole situation seem even worse. Even if we deal with all the Healers in this town, that's just the beginning. But for now, we need to focus on the children. Time's running out for them.

"There's five of us so let's take twenty pills each," I

suggest. "Then Ryker will assign each of us a cat who will guide us to shifter children that are sick. Now that we know – well, assume – that it doesn't matter how long ago they ate the sweets, it doesn't matter whether they're sick already or not. Let's just hope that we won't run out of pills."

"Somehow, I can't believe that there are more than a hundred children with shifter heritage," Lennox says. "At least not ones that haven't been snatched by the Pack, and those are unlikely to have been able to get any of the free sweets. Despite them giving some of the kids to the Healers for experimentation, they can't afford to get rid of their slaves."

He spits out the last word, and my neck begins to itch where I once wore my collar. Yes, he's right. The Pack relies on shifters to do their dirty work. They'd be nothing without us.

Gryphon gets up. "What are we waiting for? Let's hand out those pills before it's too late."

SAVING LIVES FEELS SURPRISINGLY GOOD. YES, TAKING lives is fun too, but this feeling goes deeper. With every pill I give to a child, my heart feels a little lighter.

The cat that's guiding me is called Haru, and he looks a bit like a miniature version of myself. Black as the night, slender and intense green eyes that take in everything around him. Together, we run through the traders' quarter, and he meows whenever he can scent a shifter child. Most of them have fallen ill already, and to my surprise, not a single parent questions me offering them a blue pill. Few of them are shifters themselves, so I assume one of their ancestors was. The poison must affect children with even just a small connection to the shifter gene. Most of them will probably never be able to shift, but the Healers were willing to kill them nonetheless.

With every child we see, my hate for the Fangs grows. In one case, we're too late; the boy literally takes his last breath while we arrive at his front door. It's heart-breaking, but there's no time to stop and think about what a waste the loss of such a young life is.

When Haru no longer finds any children in the trader's quarter, we move to one of the wealthier districts. There are only two shifter children there, both of them vomiting heavily. Just in time.

We never stay to see the antidote take effect. I just hope it does. That this isn't all for nothing, raising parents' hopes.

To make sure, we return to the very first house once I've given away all my twenty pills. The little girl, no older than five, is looking remarkably better, her cheeks no longer as pale. Her mother smothers me with hugs, and I more or less run out of the door to avoid being hugged to death.

Too early for that joke? Yes, maybe. Blame it on my cold assassin heart that isn't all that cold any longer. In fact, it's bleeding heavily. The only thing that makes it better is to know that we saved lives today. We killed, we fought, we helped. Maybe that should become Meow's new motto.

Or even better: Meow. *We're not afraid of you, Fangs. We're going to come for you, and we will destroy you. We're going to avenge the children you killed and will make sure you won't be able to ever repeat this somewhere else.*

There. Quite a mouthful for a tagline, but who cares. I certainly don't.

EPILOGUE

Lily and I are in my bedroom, enjoying some butter biscuits I got from a bakery on the way back. I decided we'd earned ourselves a treat. Saving seventy-two children from certain death deserves a reward.

We sit there in comfortable silence, munching on our biscuits. After all the rush and excitement of the past few days, it feels good to just relax.

"This isn't over yet, is it," Lily suddenly says. It's not a question. She knows that it's true.

"No, it isn't." I sigh. "We've only stopped them from doing this here, but who knows if anyone is conducting the same experiments in other places? For all we know, they could be more advanced already. They could have killed hundreds of shifter children without us knowing."

Lily shudders. "We need to do something, Kat. We can't just ignore what the Fangs are doing. I know they're dangerous, but now that we've seen even a fraction of their plans, I don't think I can ever go back to how we were before."

I don't reply. I've had the same thoughts. As much as I miss the old days of killing and enjoying my assassin's life, the world has turned a lot darker since I accepted the Kindler case. I almost wish I'd never done that. Sometimes, ignorance is bliss.

"We'll have to be careful," I say eventually. "We're likely on their radar now. I'm sure they're going to send people here to find out what happened. Losing most of their local operatives in one night won't go unnoted."

My friend nods. "And we'll be ready. We have more knowledge now than we had before. Lennox found all these documents that might help us discover more about how far their influence really stretches. We may not be as organised and powerful as the Fangs, but we have hearts."

I laugh. "I never thought I'd think of that as an advantage."

"Me neither. Being a cold-hearted assassin always seemed easy. Bringing emotions into the game makes things harder."

She's right about that. And not just because I feel sad about the shifter children, especially Mystery Man's granddaughter. Also because I now have two new people on the team. Two men who I haven't quite decided what to feel about. Lennox, the old friend who took me on a not-date with flowers. Gryphon, the assassin who's almost as good at killing as me. Who I somehow seem to recognise myself in.

I need to guard my feelings well. I can't afford to get emotional. Too much is at stake.

"There's something else," Lily says and gets up,

walking towards the window. It's getting late and the last birds are about to finish their evening songs. I join her, intrigued by what's bothering my friend.

"I'm not quite sure how to say this, Kat," Lily begins, staring out towards the sunset. "You know how I tested Ryker's blood?"

I nod. "Is something wrong with him? Is he sick?"

"No, not exactly. He's… well, he's not a cat."

I can't help but laugh. "Are you drunk? I reassure you, he most definitely is a cat. You've seen him. Four legs, shiny fur, whiskers, an arrogant frown. He's a cat. No doubt about that."

"He's not *just* a cat," Lily blurts. "He's a shifter. Ryker is a shifter."

~ The End ~

Meow! I hope you enjoyed this book! If you did, please leave a review and tell others about Meow. The more readers she has, the more Kat will purr.

The next book in this series will be <u>Scratch</u>, where we'll find out more about the Fangs and about Kat's new companions. And yes, Ryker really isn't just a cat.

ALSO BY

Daughter of Winter Series (Paranormal reverse harem)

Winter Princess

Winter Heiress

Winter Queen

Winter Goddess

\>> Box set

Mother of Gods (prequel)

Demon's Revenge (spin-off)

Samhain Goddess (spin-off in an anthology)

Seven Wardens (Paranormal RH co-written with Laura Greenwood)

From the Deeps

Into the Mists

Beneath the Earth

Within the Flames

Above the Waves

Under the Ice

Rule the Dark

Prequel: Beyond the Loch

Spin-off: Through the Storms

Claiming Her Bears (Dystopian bear shifter RH)

Polar Destiny

Polar Fates

Polar Miracle

The Mars Diaries (Sci-fi RH linked to the Drowning series)

Alone

Hidden

Found

\>>Box Set

Defiance (contemporary dark RH)

Abandoned Heart

Broken Princess

Stolen Soul

Infernal Descent (paranormal RH based on Dante's Inferno, co-written with Bea Paige)

Hell's Calling

Hell's Weeping

Hell's Burning

Catnip Assassins (urban fantasy)

Meow

Scratch

Purrr

Anthologies and Box Sets

Hungry for More – charity cookbook

Captivated – contains my post-apocalyptic shifter RH Three Arrows

ABOUT THE AUTHOR

Skye MacKinnon is a USA Today Bestselling Author with a slight obsession with bunnies, dried mango and Scotland. And when she says slight... her friends are trying to find ways to trick her into not having a book set in Scotland.

Whether it's set in space (Scottish space, obviously), fantasy worlds (Scottish fantasy worlds, obviously), or Scotland, Skye's tales are full of magic, romance and adventure. Oh, and unicorns. There's a few demons, too.

Follow her on social media:

Newsletter: skyemackinnon.com/newsletter/

Website: skyemackinnon.com/

Twitter: twitter.com/skye_mackinnon/

Facebook: facebook.com/skyemackinnonauthor/

Facebook group: facebook.com/groups/skyesbookharem/

Instagram: instagram.com/skyemackinnonauthor/

Bookbub: bookbub.com/authors/skye-mackinnon

Pinterest: pinterest.co.uk/skyemackinnonauthor/

Printed in Great Britain
by Amazon